Night Breed
Immortal Destiny

Lorraine Kennedy

Copyright @ 2011 Lorraine Kennedy

All Rights Reserved

ISBN-13: 978-1463793111

ISBN-10: 1463793111

Books in Print by Lorraine Kennedy

Realm of the Wolf Series

Wolf Dance
Moon Calling

Immortal Destiny Series

Born to Darkness
Night Breed

Chapter One

When she inhaled, the heat scorched the tender flesh of her throat and lungs. Flames leaped at the thick fabric of her skirt. Soon her clothes would catch fire and sear the flesh beneath the fabric. She could already feel the heat, but she refused to cry out. Staring out at the crowd gathered around her, she mentally cursed all that were present. Their bloodthirsty eyes gazed in her direction, waiting for the instant that she would take her last breath.

He stood apart from the crowd, hidden in the shadows. She did not need to see him, she knew who he was. Even now, she could hear his dark whispers promising her immortality, if she would accept his poisonous kiss.

Her skirt caught fire. The flesh of her legs sizzled and blistered - the excruciating pain quickly chasing away her will to live.

"Burn witch … burn!" The crowd chanted over and over.

"May God have mercy on your soul." The clergyman's voice was weak, drowned out by the angry - unforgiving crowd.

Gasping for air, Sarah's eyes flew open. The blankets were tangled around her legs, and for a brief moment she panicked, believing that she was still tied to the wooden stake. She frantically tore away the blankets so that she could examine her legs for burns, but there was no evidence of the blisters that had been there in her nightmare.

Taking a deep breath, she fell back into her pillow and closed her eyes.

It was stress.

She had been under too much stress. The last week of spring semester had been hell and now the stress was catching up with her.

With that thought in mind, Sarah tried to drift off to sleep. Just as she started to relax, the double windows burst open and a strong wind blew through the room. She sat up and stared in the direction of the windows. The wind tore at the lavender curtains, shredding one panel and nearly pulling it off the curtain rod.

Slipping out from beneath the covers, Sarah went to the window. The full moon was obscured by the storm clouds that had gathered over the sea.

"Saraaah," a faint voice called out to her from the dark.

Sarah held her breath, waiting to see if she would hear the voice again.

Had it been her imagination?

"Saraaah." The soft male voice seemed to drift on the wind.

Leaning out the window, she peered into the darkness below, but could see no one. Nothing seemed out of place in her aunt's perfectly manicured gardens. Another burst of wind drove her back from the window.

Pushing against the gale, Sarah forced the window closed. Giving up on sleep she slipped on her robe. Maybe if she did some reading, she could relax enough to fall asleep.

Just as she came to the conclusion that she hadn't really heard anything at all, the windows again flew open.

"Saraaah." The whispering voice seemed to be one with the wind.

Stepping to the window, Sarah was startled when she saw a figure lurking in the shadows. The man stood near the hedge maze, not in full sight, but was not exactly hidden either. He stared up at her - a strange light burning in his eyes.

He was beautiful, but dark. Even from where she stood at the window she could feel the danger. A sense of foreboding settled around her like a heavy cloak. Sarah's first thought was that it was her time and the angel of death had come for her. Then she thought that he might be a dark specter - a lost soul searching for the light.

Even before the thought had completely formed, she could feel his amusement at what she was thinking. He was not an angel of any kind, but he was there for her. Sarah's sixth sense picked this up so strongly that it took her breath away. She tried to back away from the window, but her legs had a will of their own and she could not get them to move.

Then she was no longer seeing the garden. She was seeing his face, staring at her - angry, but yet he seemed to be pleading with her. She was lying on a bed, wrapped in his arms. He was pleading with her for something - something that she could not bring herself to do. The vision was more like a memory that she just could not completely grasp. For a brief instant, she felt compelled to go to him - to touch him.

As soon as the thought entered her mind, she banished it - slamming the door on it as if the very idea was too terrifying to contemplate. The dark figure bowed to her and then disappeared into the darkness.

* * * *

Darrien walked away.

It would have been easy to rise upon the winds and take her from the window - to steal away her last breath and extract the life force that flowed through her veins, but he couldn't do it. Not yet.

The sight of her standing at the window was tantalizing. The way the wind blew through her long - auburn hair, and her silk nightgown fluttering behind her like the wings of an angel had stirred a desire deep within him. The image was enchanting, inflaming his hunger - his lust for blood, and his lust for something more. He could have taken her then, if not for the intrusion of the memories - memories that he had banished long ago. The pain of those memories was fresh once again, and it brought out the anguish that festered in his soul.

But why?
Why was he thinking of her now?
He had a job to do.

Darrien had discovered a long time ago, that for the vampire, nothing mattered but the moment, at least if you wanted to remain sane.

His thoughts returned to the girl. She had resisted his calling, but she would not hold out for long.

* * * *

Sarah descended the long - spiral staircase to the first floor. The scent of breakfast made her stomach growl. When she entered the kitchen, Aunt Jeanie was standing at the stove, flipping pancakes.

As usual, her aunt was wearing her red hair in a bun on top of her head, and a loose fitting black dress. "I hope you're hungry. I've made you a huge breakfast."

"Thank you auntie." Sarah kissed her cheek.

Sarah looked around the large kitchen, as if she was seeing it for the first time. She had been away at school for most of the year, and the one thing that she'd missed most about home was Aunt Jeanie's kitchen. The kitchen's large windows let in an abundance of morning sunshine. During the warmer months, they would often eat breakfast with the windows open so they could enjoy the tangy sea air.

"Have a seat." Jeanie placed a plate full of pancakes on the table.

Sarah sat down and took a bite. Though the food was delicious, she barely tasted it. Finally Jeanie heaved her heavy frame into the chair across from her.

"What's on your mind Sarah? You have been playing with your food more than eating it."

"There was a man ... or something ... standing in the garden last night."

Aunt Jeanie drew her brows together. "What do you mean, or something?"

"I don't think he was human." Sarah set her fork on her plate. She couldn't get another bite down until she figured out who or what had called her to her window in the middle of the night.

"I don't know. He almost didn't seem real, and his eyes had this ... strange light in them, but I don't think he was a ghost either."

Aunt Jeanie stared at her, a look of shock spreading across her face. "A light in his eyes you say?"

Sarah nodded. "Whoever he was, there was something dark about him."

"Hmm, well you stay clear of him."

"Is he real ... or something else?" Sarah asked.

Growing up in Aunt Jeanie's house, she'd become accustomed to things being a little strange. The Fabre family had practiced witchcraft for centuries, and Aunt Jeanie was no different. Sarah had been able to see spirits since she was a child, but she could usually tell if the person she was seeing was living, or dead.

"Oh he's probably real enough," Jeanie said, as she got to her feet and started cleaning up breakfast.

"Well?" Sarah wanted her aunt to continue, but it appeared as if Jeanie had said all that she intended to say on the matter.

"The summer solstice is this month." Jeanie gave her a wink. "Maybe we'll pick up this conversation after that."

Sarah leaned back in her chair and folded her arms in front of her. "I'm not so sure I'll be going."

"Oh fiddlesticks! Of course you're going." Jeanie waved the suggestion away as if it were the most absurd thing she'd ever heard. "You are probably one of the most talented of the Fabre women in generations. Why wouldn't you join us?"

"Maybe I just want normal! I've never had normal until I went away to school. Everyone in this town thinks we are freaks. The Sutter Point witches!" Sarah scowled.

"Normal is far too overrated," Jeanie assured her.

Sarah decided it was best to drop the subject for now. Later she would talk with her aunt about moving to Portland permanently. There was time. She still had a couple of years before she'd get her degree.

* * * *

Sarah stood beneath the large - wraparound porch and stared out at the ocean. The sound of the surf crashing against the rocks was soothing and exhilarating at the same time. If she moved away, she would miss waking in the morning and listening to the sea just outside her bedroom window. But could she survive if she didn't?

Sutter Point was a dark shadow that hovered over her life, but when she'd gone away to Portland to attend the university, that shadow had been lifted. It wasn't Aunt Jeanie's fault. Jeanie was the sweetest aunt ever. No, it was because no one knew her in Portland - no one knew of the Fabre witches.

Closing her eyes, Sarah thought of the day that she'd come to live in Sutter Point. Though it was long ago, she could still remember it as if it were yesterday. Her mom's green eyes - misty with tears, and how she'd knelt down to tell Sarah goodbye.

"I'll be back soon peanut," Beth told her, kissing her daughter's forehead.

Sarah shook her head. "I want to go with you mommy! Don't leave me!"

"You'll love your Aunt Jeanie," Beth assured her. "Jeanie and I … we would have such fun as girls. We would sneak treats in the middle of the night and go sit on the beach. The two of us would spend hours just talking. Jeanie was my best friend … and she'll be your best friend too."

"But mom, I just want to stay with you!" Sarah whimpered.

Beth smiled. "I know you do sweetheart. But where I'm going would be much too dangerous for a little girl."

Her mother had never come back for her. Aunt Jeanie had done her best to ease Sarah's hurt and anger at being abandoned by her mother, but the pain had never really gone away.

Day after day, Sarah would ask about her mother, but Aunt Jeanie never had any answers for her. She could tell that it was nearly as painful for her aunt as it was for her, so eventually Sarah had quit asking. She loved Aunt Jeanie and didn't want to cause her grief, but the pain still festered in Sarah.

Why hadn't her mom come back for her?

Sarah opened her eyes, willing the memory away.

From behind, she heard Aunt Jeanie clearing her throat. Sarah turned to look at her.

"Are you okay honey?"

Sarah forced a smile to her lips. "Yes, I'm fine auntie."

"Well okay." Jeanie didn't seem convinced. "Do you feel up to digging some clams for dinner?"

"Sure. I'll get on it now," Sarah promised.

Jeanie stared at the sinking sun. "Just hurry. You don't want to be out after dark."

* * * *

Staring at the computer screen, Ethan tapped his fingers across his desk. Nicole looked up from the book she was reading.

"Really Ethan, you are making it difficult to concentrate. What's on your mind?"

"I just can't believe that girl on the coast was a miss!" he said, shaking his head. "I was so sure that she was one of them."

Nicole had to agree with him. Cassie had seemed to fit the profile, and it was rumored that her family may have had some involvement with vampirism in the past, but it had been just rumor. The girl and her family were as normal as you could get.

"Well ... you still think that the girl we are looking for is on the coast?"

Ethan nodded. "According to my source."

"Well why doesn't this source just come out and tell us who and where she is?"

"I don't think he knows for sure, and he cannot interfere with the immortals too much, or he risks a war between his kind and ours."

Nicole bit at her bottom lip. "If Omar finds her before we do ... " Her words trailed off when Dash stepped through the open office door.

Dash took a seat in front of Nicole's desk. "What ... you talking about those mysterious vanishing sisters?"

She nodded. "Were you listening at the door?" she asked with a half smile.

Dash put his thumb and index finger together. "Well maybe just a bit."

Nicole rolled her eyes.

"I've heard that Omar has found one of them, and he has sent an assassin to take care of her. At least that's the whisperings among the vamps," he told them.

"Oh no!" Nicole felt her heart skip a beat. "Are they saying where she is?" she asked.

"Nope."

"This is why it would have been best if Alec had not revealed his opposition to Omar. He could have gotten this information."

"Well he wasn't given a lot of choice," Nicole reminded Ethan.

"Where is that dark sadistic lover of yours anyway?" Dash asked, the amusement obvious in his voice. Dash never missed an opportunity to let her know how odd it was that her lover was a vampire.

Nicole didn't care. Alec was the light in her soul, it didn't matter what others thought. Thinking of Alec made her crave his touch. She really missed hearing the sound of his voice, especially when she was feeling down. Every moment away from him was like an eternity.

"Romania," she told Dash, trying to force her thoughts into another direction. Thinking of Alec was too hard when he was so far away.

"No kidding! He actually left you here alone?"

Nicole smiled. "He knew you and Ethan would look after me. And let's not forget the ever watchful eye of my father."

"But Romania! That's a bit old school isn't it?"

"There is an ancient manuscript that has been hidden away, and it supposedly tells the story of our species. Alec is searching for it," Ethan explained.

"Your father already knows these things. Why are we chasing after old manuscripts?" Dash asked her, narrowing his eyes.

"Maybe so, but he thinks that we are not ready to hear about these secrets. He doesn't know that Alec went to search for this book."

Dash whistled, shaking his head. "You two are really out to piss your father off!"

Nicole smiled. Her father had been furious when Alec returned to New Orleans, and even more enraged when Nicole put down the law. She'd told her father that unless she had his blessing to be with Alec, she would go away with him and never return. Donavan had given in reluctantly, but not without a promise from Alec that he would always put Nicole's safety first.

"My father believes that the truth would be too destructive … to all species on earth."

Dash shook his head. "He's a vampire! Doesn't he know that it's not his duty to worry about the fate of earth's population?"

Nicole lifted her shoulders. "We have other things to worry about right now, like how we are going to find my sister." Nicole shuddered to think of what might happen if this assassin got to her sister before they did.

Chapter Two

Sarah felt his presence. She felt him watching her before she lifted her eyes from the wet sand to see him standing near the dark - gray cliffs behind her. The breeze played with his wavy brown hair, blowing it into his face to hide his eyes - those strange alluring eyes.

She had been so engrossed in her thoughts as she pulled clams from the sand that she'd failed to see how far the sun had set. It was now only a red sliver over the dark waters of the Pacific. Sarah quickly picked up the pail that held the harvested clams, and the small hand shovel that she'd been using. Getting to her feet, she started for the path that wound around the steep cliffs. Her aunt's house was situated at the top of these cliffs. The impressive structure was like a sentry standing watch over the sea.

Sarah took a quick peek at the man from the corner of her eye. She saw that he still stood near the cliffs - still watching her. He was sticking to the shadows. Every few seconds, he would glance at the sun and then look back in her direction. Sarah tried to walk faster, but she wasn't going to make it to the path before the sun had completely vanished from the horizon.

One moment he was standing in the shadows, and the next instant he was blocking her path. He moved so quickly that she barely had time to blink.

Sarah stopped and looked up at his face. Now that she was so close to him, his presence was overwhelming. He was so beautiful - so enchanting that it took her breath away to be near him.

"Excuse me," Sarah muttered, when she was finally able to find her voice.

He didn't move, but continued to stare at her. She had to look away to keep from drowning in those fascinating eyes.

Sarah waited, but he would not let her pass. Stepping to the side, she tried to walk around him, but again he blocked her way.

"Do you mind?" Sarah's anger was simmering. As long as she could grasp that anger and not look into his eyes, she would be fine.

"Sarah ... is that your name?" he asked in a deep - silky voice.

"What do you want?" she would not raise her eyes to look at his face, nor would she answer his question.

"Just to talk ... that's all." He placed his fingers beneath her chin and forced her to look at him.

His brown eyes burned with hunger - a hunger that pervaded her senses, sending fear straight into her heart. Sarah took a step back.

For just a second, a look of confusion entered his eyes and they lost their power over her. Sarah took the opportunity to run, but the sand made her progress slow - painfully slow.

Then he was there again, knocking her to the ground. The pail flew out of her hands and the clams spilled onto the sand. He was lying on her - his face only inches from hers. Again she was pulled into his eyes. Sarah fought to break free of his hold, but her struggles were in vain. He was much too strong.

His eyes glowed with an inner light that drew her in and terrified her at the same time. He drew back his lips to reveal long - white fangs. Sarah panicked, her mind screaming the unbelievable truth that this was not a man at all, but a vampire. She would succumb to a creature of the night.

Squeezing her eyes shut, she waited for his teeth to pierce the artery in her neck, but the seconds passed and she felt no teeth - no pain. Sarah opened her eyes. He was still staring at her, but his eyes had lost the ravenous look of a moment ago, and his fangs were no longer visible.

The look in his eyes was soft, almost whimsical. Sarah was startled when she felt his cool lips against hers, and even more surprised to feel her body responding to his touch. His tongue was in her mouth and he was kissing her, but his kiss was so demanding - so voracious that it was frightening. Despite her fear, she wanted him to kiss her. Sarah's heart craved his kiss - her soul knew his touch.

Sarah wrapped her arms around his neck, returning his kiss with a passion that matched his. When he pulled back to look down at her, she saw a deep pain in his eyes that tugged at her heart.

He got to his feet and started to walk away. He was going to leave her there in the sand - longing for his touch.

"Wait a minute!" she called after him. "Who are you?"

He continued walking, refusing to turn and look at her.

Sarah got to her feet and ran after him. "Who are you? What is it that you want?" she asked, breathless from running to catch up with him.

Slowing his pace, he looked over at her. "I came here to kill you."

Stopping in her tracks, Sarah stared after him in stunned silence.

He seemed to be waiting for her to say something, but she couldn't find any words.

"You need to run Sarah. Run as far away from here as you can get ... run far away from *me!*"

"Why didn't you do it then? Why didn't you kill me?" she asked.

He stared at her for a long time. "I don't know," he told her. Turning away, he started walking again.

"At least tell me your name." She fell into step beside him.

He stopped suddenly, and when he looked at her she saw fury leap from his dark eyes. "Did you not hear me? I was sent here to kill you. You should be running away from me, not following me!"

Sarah stopped and watched him walk away.

What was wrong with her anyway?

He had just admitted that he was going to kill her, and she was still chasing after him. Even more bizarre than this was the fact that she actually wanted him to come back.

* * * *

Sarah took what clams that she'd been able to save and dumped them into the kitchen sink so that they could be cleaned. Aunt Jeanie watched her with open curiosity. Her aunt was smart. She had always been good at picking up other people's thoughts and feelings. Sarah had never been very good at hiding things from Aunt Jeanie.

"He came for you again," Jeanie stated.

"He is a vampire." Sarah turned from the sink to look at her aunt. "Is that one of the big secrets that I'm not permitted to know? That there are vampires?"

Her aunt clucked her tongue. "Girl, you do look for the sinister in everything."

Sarah shook her head. "I just want to know who he is and why he came here to kill me. That's what he said ... that he came here to kill me."

"You do remember that I told you to be back before dark," Jeanie said, shaking a finger at her.

"Do you know who he is?" Sarah asked.

"What did he look like?" Jeanie asked as she stepped over to the sink to start the task of shelling and cleaning the clams.

"He had brown hair ... about to here," Sarah said, pointing to the top of her shoulders. "And he had brown eyes. He was a lot taller than me."

"Well it doesn't sound like the one I thought it might be."

"Who is it that you are talking about? What about this vampire thing? I've seen some strange things, but vampires? Really?" Sarah was getting impatient.

"There are some things that you just don't understand yet," her aunt explained while she attended to the clams, running cold water over them.

When she was done, she dried her hands on a dishtowel and flung it over the towel holder. "Come and let's have a chat." Jeanie grabbed Sarah's arm and led her to the kitchen table. "How about a nice cup of lavender tea?"

Without waiting for a reply, Jeanie stepped over to the stove and put the teapot on to cook. When the pot started whistling, she removed it from the stove and poured the tea into two cups. After setting a cup in front of Sarah, Jeanie took the chair opposite of her.

"Sarah, you've lived among witches long enough to know that things are not always what they seem."

Sarah nodded but said nothing.

"Though most people can't see them, there are always spirits around us. Sometimes when that picture falls off of the wall, or a glass is knocked from a table, it isn't just an accident. But you already know this stuff don't you?"

"I know auntie, but vampires?"

"Like I said, there are many things in this world that you simply are not aware of, but that doesn't make them any less real."

"Why do you think he wanted to kill me?"

"That's another question." Jeanie placed a finger to her cheek, which she often did when she was thinking. "More importantly, why didn't he kill you?"

"I asked him. He told me that he didn't know why he didn't do it. And then he just left."

"Vampires! They're a secretive bunch. You could go through your whole life and never even know that they existed. Chances are, if you did run across one, you would not live to tell about it, which makes this situation all the more curious."

"I want to find out who he is?"

Jeanie looked over at her niece with narrowed eyes. "Now tell me why do you need to know that? I would think you would be more concerned with the why ... than the who?"

"There was something about him. Something almost familiar." Sarah tried to explain what she couldn't understand herself.

"Hmm." A look of concern clouded her dark green eyes. "It's settled. You must join us for Midsummer's Eve. You will need the protection of the coven."

How could Sarah argue with this? Even the one that had come to kill her had basically told her that she was still in danger.

"Do you remember Clyde from the fishery?" Jeanie asked, changing the subject abruptly.

Sarah nodded.

"Well you know he passed away and his viewing is tonight?"

"Yes, I heard that. Are you going?" she asked her aunt.

"The family was wondering that since you were in town and all ... maybe you could come and visit after the viewing? You know ... like you would do for some of the people in town when you were younger?"

Sarah drew her brows together. What her aunt was asking was if she would go to the viewing and see if she could communicate with the deceased. Sarah had been able to communicate with the dead for as long as she could remember.

While growing up, some of the locals would frequently ask her to attend viewings so that they could have one last conversation with their loved one. Her talent was often misunderstood. She could not contact the dead at will. They chose when and where, or even if they would communicate with her. But the one place that they would almost certainly be present, was their own funeral. The thought of attending a viewing or a funeral made her feel sick.

It's not that Sarah minded helping the bereaved. It was just that when you touched death too often, it had a way of creeping into your life in unexpected ways. This was why she'd turned her back on the craft and everything paranormal. You never knew when something or someone might come back to haunt you.

Jeanie reached out and covered Sarah's hand with her own. "What happened to Gina was an accident. You know that don't you?" Jeanie asked, reading Sarah's thoughts.

Gina had been her best friend growing up. During their first year of high school they'd gone to a beach party with a few of the locals. It was that night that Sarah came face to face with death in a very personal way.

Though Sarah tried to talk her out of it, Gina went into the water anyway. She wasn't the only one that had gone into the water that night, but she was the only one that did not come back.

They blamed Sarah for it. She talked to the dead and brought death to those around her. The kids teased her mercilessly. She should have hated them for it, but maybe it was true.

There had been a warning that morning that something would happen. She'd gone into the bathroom at school. Quickly slipping in there to brush her hair before the next class, because the wind had made such a mess of it.

One minute she had been looking at her own reflection, and the next she'd seen Gina all bloated and gray, staring at her with her dead eyes. It had been a warning from the other side. She'd tried to tell Gina that she had a strange feeling about going out that night, but her friend wouldn't listen.

Jeanie snapped her fingers. "Have you been listening to me?" she asked Sarah.

"I'm sorry. I didn't hear what you said."

"They said that it's really important. Besides, it would give you a chance to brush up on your skills," Jeanie added.

Sarah wanted to say no, but Clyde had always been nice to them whenever they went to the docks to buy fish. She decided that she'd do it for Clyde's sake. It would give her a chance to say goodbye.

Sarah gave her aunt a weak smile. "Okay,' she agreed.

* * * *

Hidden in the large oak, Darrien watched her through the kitchen windows. From the expression on her face it was obvious that she was upset, but she seemed to be surrounded by some kind of force that kept him from probing her mind. He could sense her, but he couldn't read her thoughts.

Why couldn't he bring himself to snuff out her life?

He'd been so close to doing just that. To sinking his teeth into her flesh and drinking of her sweet nectar. Her fear had been tantalizing, inflaming his hunger even more, but then the memories came back. The memories of another human – another enchanting witch, weaving her spell over him until he was mad with desire. But in the end, she had refused eternity. She had chosen death instead, leaving him to endure an endless existence without her.

While she had loved him, she had also hated what he was. She'd hated him for what he'd done.

If only the witch could have forgiven him. How could he have known what she would become to him, and that she would eventually extract a revenge on him more tormenting than an eternity in the fiery pits of hell? Loving a woman that had been dead for over two hundred years, was a fate worse than any hell that man could dream up.

Since the night that she'd left this world, his soul had known no light. With a heart so black, it was little wonder that he was known among vampires to show no mercy to his victims. But then he'd peered into Sarah's terrified eyes - eyes so green they appeared to have captured the stormy sea within their depths. There had been that flicker of light that touched his heart, and he had been unable to take her life.

But they would send others!

Someone would come and do what he had been unable to do. Her very existence was forbidden. She was a danger to the ancients. Their world would only go on as it had, if they could be rid of the sisters.

Darrien had been selected for this task because he was so ruthless. What would Omar do when he realized that his chosen assassin had failed? What would he do when they sent someone else to finish the job?

When Omar had sent him to eliminate the witch, he hadn't known that she was a Fabre witch.

Would it have made a difference if he'd known?

Somehow Darrien doubted it. It might have made all the difference a couple hundred years go, but not today. At least it hadn't until that moment that he'd been ready to take her life, and found that he couldn't do it.

Ascending into the dark sky, Darrien let his hunger guide him to his prey, like he had every night for centuries, but tonight he would do so with less enthusiasm. The hunt didn't seem quite as alluring as it had before - before he had lost himself in those beautiful - bewitching eyes.

* * * *

Sarah and Jeanie waited outside the funeral home until they saw the people begin to leave. The funeral was to be tomorrow. Tonight, friends and family would have one last opportunity to view the deceased before the coffin was closed.

"You ready for this?" Jeanie gave her an encouraging smile.

Nodding, Sarah followed her aunt through the parking lot to the large double glass doors of the mortuary. Like every time she came to one of these places, Sarah felt an ache in her stomach, and with each step she took, the pain grew worse. She knew it was anxiety, but was at a loss for how to control it.

Jeanie led her into the viewing room where Clyde's family was waiting for them. The metallic gray coffin was positioned between two large flower arrangements. Resting on the top of the coffin was a spray of white roses. The oppressive atmosphere of the funeral home tightened the knot in her stomach. The grief around her was overwhelming. It was like a black fog encircling her, finding its way into her mouth and nose to cut off her breath. She felt as if it would smother her until she was as lifeless as the body within the coffin.

Over the years, Sarah had come to dread these occasions. The one thing that she had discovered was that the dead were far easier to deal with than the living.

Sarah would not go to the coffin and peer in at the body of the old man. She knew that Clyde was no longer in the shell that had once been his body. No, Clyde wasn't in there at all. At the moment, the old man was standing next to his wife.

Mrs. Morris was inconsolable. Someone was asking Clyde's wife a question, but all she could do was shake her head while she sobbed into a white tissue. Clyde was standing next to his wife, trying to talk to her, but of course Mrs. Morris wasn't aware that he was even there.

Though Clyde was now in spirit, he appeared exactly as he had every time Sarah had seen him. He had on a black cap and blue overalls. He was still wearing the rubber boots he would wear at work to keep from getting fish guts on his shoes. His hair was completely gray, as was his mustache. To Sarah, Clyde still looked like he was among the living.

Clyde glanced over and saw Sarah standing by the viewing room doors. Leaving his wife's side, he drifted over to Sarah and her aunt. "Thank heaven you're here! Will you tell this woman to stop her crying and listen to me?"

Sarah smiled sadly, shaking her head. "Clyde, she can't hear you now. You've passed away."

"Well I know that! Otherwise I wouldn't be standing in this godforsaken corpse mill," he frowned.

Mrs. Morris noticed Sarah and came running over to her. "Oh dear girl! I'm so glad you could make it. Can you contact Mr. Morris for me? You know … he has all of the passwords to our online accounts and the fool never gave them to me."

Sarah looked over at Clyde. He appeared to be somewhat confused.

"Well?" she asked.

He shook his head. "Tell her I forgot them myself."

"He doesn't remember what they are," she told Mrs. Morris.

The old woman frowned. "Well a lot of help he is."

Clyde held up his hand. "Oh wait a minute! Tell her I did write them down on a piece of a paper and hid it in one of the couch cushions."

Sarah relayed the message to Mrs. Morris, who seemed relieved, but had gone back to crying in her tissue. "Tell him I'm mad as hell that he went and had that heart attack … just before he was going to take me to Seattle for our anniversary."

"He can hear you," she told the woman.

Clyde shook his head. "Tell her I'm sorry, and that she should still go and celebrate our time together."

Again, Sarah relayed the message before turning back to Clyde. The old man's attention seemed to have wandered. He was peering to his side, seeing something that was invisible to Sarah. She assumed it was the light and he was ready to cross over, but Clyde once again turned to Sarah.

"Gina wants to know why you ignore her?"

Sarah gasped. Gina was the one person that she had never been able to communicate with. She hadn't heard a peep from her friend.

"I can't see her … or hear her," Sarah told him.

Aunt Jeanie put a protective arm around Sarah.

"She wants you to know that if you don't run now, you will be seeing her soon," Clyde told her.

Sarah stood there in shock, her mouth wide open.

"Your friend wants you to know that if you close yourself off, she can't help you."

Sarah shut her eyes and tried to concentrate, but she just couldn't pick up on Gina's presence.

Giving up, she opened her eyes, but Clyde had vanished.

"He's gone," she told Jeanie and Mrs. Morris.

"The man always did have a habit of leaving without saying goodbye. Thank you for coming dear." Mrs. Morris moved back to the group of family members that were waiting for her near the casket.

"We should get home," Jeanie said, taking Sarah by the arm.

"Run Sarah!" The voice vibrated through the room, shaking the chandelier.

No one seemed to notice but Sarah.

The vampire had told her to run, and now Gina. Where could she run to, and whom was she running from?

Chapter Three

As eerie as the ancient cemetery was, the blanket of swirling fog hugging the ground made it even more so. Alec stood at the edge of the graveyard. Behind him, a long abandoned village church and hundreds of gravestones rose up from the night mist. They were a reminder to all that life was short, and that sooner or later death would come for them. It would come for everyone but Alec, and his kind.

Alec's soul was damned to prey upon the living for all time. Nicole was his saving grace, but for how long would that last? Sooner or later, Omar would manage to turn her or kill her? Maybe she would escape Omar, but she would not escape time. He would once again walk the earth alone, unless he could free himself of his curse.

He was sure that the ancients knew how to do this. They knew how the vampire could live in the light and exist without the need to prey on the living for their blood.

Alec stared up at the massive black cliffs. At the very top was a fortress that had occupied the same imposing stance for hundreds of years. Castle Arges stood watch over the empty village nearby. This was how the master of Castle Arges preferred it. Solitude was the vampire's friend, especially in Romania, a land of legends and vampires.

Here in this dark land, it was difficult for the vampire to hide. The people were always watchful for these creatures, but few dared to confront Luciano. Some believed that Luciano was the oldest of the ancients, and perhaps even the first vampire, but Alec didn't believe this. He did not doubt that Luciano was one of the ancients, but not the first.

A steep staircase led to the top of the cliffs and Castle Arges, but Alec needed no stairs. Slowly he rose out of the mist and flew through the night toward Luciano's haven of darkness.

Confronting Luciano was a fool's mission and Alec, was no fool. He would search out the castle himself for the Book of Anu. More than a thousand years ago, the words of an immortal were preserved in this manuscript, but it was kept well hidden by the ancients, if it actually existed at all.

Alec hoped that it did, but he'd spent two centuries searching for it, without finding even a hint that the manuscript was anything but myth. Then Lex had confirmed its existence. He was a member of the *Vilka* pack, but Alec could not help but wonder what the wolves could know of the vampires? The *Vilkas* were the wolf people of Eastern Europe, and they were ancient, but what could they really know about vampires?

The courtyard was empty and dark, the perfect place for Alec to gain entrance to Castle Arges. His feet touched down on the stone surface of the courtyard, barely making any noise at all. Normally he would have little fear of discovery, but this was no ordinary home. This was the home of Luciano, a vampire so powerful that none dared oppose him, not even Omar.

Alec slipped inside through a large wooden door. It creaked as he pulled it open, but not enough to make others aware of his presence. He found himself in a long - dimly lit corridor. Not much had changed at Castle Arges since medieval times. There was now electricity and probably running water, but it appeared almost exactly as it had all those years ago. That was one thing that you could be sure about with the ancients. They did not like change, and tended to squash anything that would bring about change, or a shifting of power.

The last time he'd been at the castle, he had not made it into the lower levels or any of the hidden passages. Alec decided that would be the best place to begin his search. A scream from another part of the castle brought Alec to a standstill. He listened for a long time. There was another shriek of agony.

Alec blocked out the sound. Someone was playing with their food. This was not the way it was supposed to be. The humans were a source of life, not a toy for cruel amusement. He continued down the corridor, and was more determined than ever to end the curse of the immortal.

* * * *

Sarah stuffed the St. John's Wort into the plastic bag and sealed it. It was her fiftieth bag in an hour. She heard the front door open and knew that her aunt was home from her weekly shopping trip into town. Aunt Jeanie loved her privacy and preferred to stay within her home, but she also liked to gossip with her friends whenever she got the chance.

Fraternizing with the others was why she made it a point to go to town each week to shop, even if they didn't really need anything. She and the other ladies would gather at the local diner for a little catching up. Of course many of the patrons of the Grotto would leave when they saw the ladies coming, but they didn't let that bother them at all. A few even found it amusing that after hundreds of years, so many of the locals still feared them.

"You've been a busy bee," Jeanie said, setting two overstuffed grocery sacks on the kitchen counter.

"I'm almost done, and then I'll start on the rosemary."

"Nonsense! You're young … it's a Saturday. You need to go out and have some fun."

"But won't it be dark soon?" Sarah raised her brows.

"There's a carnival in Sutter Point. Wouldn't that be fun? There will be plenty of people there," Jeanie pointed out. "As long as you stay with the crowd, you should be fine."

Sarah shook her head. "I don't want to go alone."

"Well of course! What fun would that be?" Jeanie patted her niece's back. "That's why I've made arrangements for Taylor to go with you."

"Taylor?" Sarah scrunched up her face. "No kidding?"

"Now Miss Sarah Fabre … don't you be inhospitable." Sarah's aunt wagged a finger at her.

Sarah smiled. "I'm a little older than that."

"Good, that's my girl. He'll be here in an hour to pick you up, so you'll probably want to start getting ready," Jeanie informed her.

It wasn't that she didn't like Taylor. It was just that he was always trying to show off what he could do, and it never failed, something would go wrong with one of his spells. Last time their families had gone on a camping trip together, Taylor did a spell to keep the mosquitoes away. Instead of keeping the mosquitoes away, their campsite had been bombarded by sparrows.

Sarah loved Aunt Jeanie dearly. She just wished that her aunt would stop trying to get her hooked up with Taylor. She was only 21 years old, and still had plenty of time to think about finding a guy.

Sarah was ready and waiting for him by the front gate when he drove up, his old truck choking and coughing. He still looked exactly the same as he did the last time she'd seen him. His sandy blond hair appeared as if he'd forgotten to comb it when he got up in the morning, but his blue eyes had a good-natured twinkle, and Sarah liked that.

There wasn't anything wrong with Taylor. He was handsome enough, in a boy next-door sort of way. He just didn't make her heart do flip-flops when she saw him. Besides, she had practically grown up with him so it would be like dating a brother.

Taylor jumped out of the truck and ran around to open the passenger door for her.

"Thanks Taylor." Sarah smiled.

When Taylor got behind the wheel, he turned and grinned at her. "Sarah, it's nice to have you back."

"Thanks, I'm happy I could come and spend some time with everyone this summer," Sarah told him, realizing that it was true. She loved Sutter Point. It was only the people that bothered her. The constant staring of the townspeople could be intolerable. Before she'd gone away to school, it got to the point that when she went out in public, her stomach would get tied up in knots. The townspeople in Sutter Point had a way of stirring Sarah's anger and bringing out the worst in her.

Taylor pulled onto the road. "Your aunt thought you could use some time away from the house."

Sarah nodded. "Yes, my auntie is always thinking of others."

Through most of the trip into town, Sarah stared silently out the window, lost in her own little world. She had so many questions, and too few answers. What had happened to her mother? Where had she gone after leaving her with Aunt Jeanie? Why wouldn't Jeanie tell her anything about her mom?

Taylor, bless his heart, seemed to sense her mood and didn't push for conversation. He wasn't her knight in shining armor, but he was a good friend.

The sun was already down. She could barely make out the thick pines to the sides of the road as they sped by them. Sarah could not help but wonder what was lurking in the dark forest. Now that she knew there really were vampires that roamed the night, undercover of darkness, she could not help but wonder what other secrets lurked within the shadows? She could almost hear her Aunt Jeanie scolding her for being so fanciful.

One moment she was staring out at the shadowy trees of the forest, and the next she was looking at his face. His eyes were there in the glass, glowing with the need to feed.

Sarah screamed. The instant she'd opened her mouth to scream, he began to fade away like mist beneath the heat of the sun. Then he was gone. There was nothing there but the woods and the darkness.

Startled, Taylor swerved. Sarah felt the truck tip to the passenger side, and she instinctively lifted her hands, pressing them against the top of the cab to brace herself. The truck rode on two tires for what seemed like an eternity, before the other side hit the road with a thud, jarring her teeth. Her heart was beating so wildly that she was sure it would burst at any moment. She held a hand against her chest, as if the gesture would somehow calm her heart.

Taylor slowed the truck and pulled off to the side of the road. "Are you okay?" he asked, visibly shaken.

Sarah nodded. "Are you?"

"Why'd you scream? You scared the crap out of me!" With his shock passing, his annoyance came through loud and clear.

A little smile touched her lips. "Aren't you the most powerful warlock in Sutter Point?" she asked, unable to resist the urge to tease him.

Taylor rolled his eyes. "Well why were you screaming your head off?"

Sarah opened her mouth to tell a little white lie, but then closed it again. Why did she feel the need to cover it up? It wasn't like they both hadn't experienced stranger things.

"I thought there was a vampire outside the window," she confessed.

The blood drained from his face. "A vampire?"

She nodded. "But maybe it was my imagination." Sarah didn't want to scare him. After all, it wasn't Taylor he was after.

Taylor reached into the dash box and pulled out a bag of salt. Without saying a word, he jumped out of the truck.

"What are you doing?" Sarah called after him.

"Getting rid of a bloodsucker!" he told her as he started sprinkling salt around the truck.

Sarah opened her door and got out. "Wait a minute. Maybe this isn't really necessary."

Taylor motioned with his hand for her to stop. "I know what I'm doing Sarah. You may want to get back inside. It's probably not safe out here."

When Taylor had circled the truck with salt, he started chanting.

"Black as night,

"Vampire take flight

"Back to the grave

"Forever from our sight."

Taylor repeated the verse three times before he stopped to look at Sarah. "That should do the trick."

"I don't know. It kind of sounded like you might have forgotten a verse. It was a little short," Sarah said with a smile.

The truth was that she really had no idea if he had done the spell right or not. She didn't know any vampire banishing spells, which was puzzling. If these creatures actually existed, why hadn't her aunt taught her any protection spells against them?

"No, I'm sure that's the one."

Sarah shrugged her shoulders and got back in the truck. Taylor did the same, sticking the salt beneath his seat. "Just in case we need it quickly," he explained.

"Oh ... okay," she smiled.

"Whoever it was shouldn't be giving us anymore trouble tonight," he told her. "You just have to know how to handle bloodsuckers."

"What do you know about vampires?"

"You know Sarah, if you took a little more interest in the craft, you'd know just how dangerous these things can be," he chastised her.

"Taylor ... what do you know?" she asked again.

"Well I know how to banish them. I know that much." He tossed her a look of reproach.

Giving up, Sarah grew quiet again. How could she find out what was going on? She didn't think that Taylor knew as much as he let on, and Sarah had the distinct feeling that Aunt Jeanie was keeping some very important information from her. Maybe she felt that until she was brought into the coven, she would not have the strength to protect herself from whatever was out there.

When they drove into the outskirts of town, Sarah felt her spirits lift at the sight of the colorful carnival lights and all the people on the streets. She'd always loved carnivals. Every summer since she'd come to live in Sutter Point, Aunt Jeanie had taken her to the carnival. Jeanie would brush off the stares as easily as she waved her hand.

She could almost hear Jeanie's voice in her head. "It doesn't matter one bit what others think of you. What matters is what you think of yourself."

As part of their yearly trip to the carnival, they'd end the day with an ice cream. By that time Sarah had already forgotten the ugly looks of the townspeople. Jeanie had a way of making the stormiest days feel like they were full of sunshine.

The carnival was being held in a large - empty lot on the edge of town. The parking lot was really a weed-choked pasture, but walking through the weeds was no big deal. At least she was getting out for a few hours.

Her aunt had been right, she really needed to see some bright lights and just have fun. The walk to the ticket booth only took a few minutes, and with so many people standing in line, Sarah didn't think anyone even noticed her.

Once inside, Taylor grabbed her hand. "Let's go on a ride."

"Okay." Sarah let him lead her toward the Asteroid Scrambler. Though this ride always gave her whiplash, she loved it. It was one of those rides that would give you an adrenaline rush that you just couldn't get enough of.

The line was short. Before long they were on the ride, and securing the safety belt around them. As the ride started moving, a lively tune began to play. Sarah grasped the bar, bracing herself so that she wouldn't be flung against Taylor. He was kicked back like he didn't have a care in the world.

Though the ride started slow enough, within seconds they were moving at a breakneck speed. Everything was a blur. The lights and the people passed by so quickly, it was almost dreamlike.

Looking over at Taylor, Sarah couldn't help but laugh at the sight of his windblown hair sticking straight up. He had lost his relaxed posture and was now holding on tightly. It felt good to laugh. She hadn't done enough of it the past few days.

Too soon the ride slowed and was over. The world was still spinning when Sarah stepped out of the little cart that they had been sitting in. She tried to focus on a large tree near the fence that surrounded the Asteroid Scrambler. As her eyes focused, she saw him leaning against the tree, staring at her.

Sarah quickly glanced at Taylor, and when she directed her eyes back to the tree, he was gone.

Had she imagined him?

"I'm hungry, let's go get some dinner." Taylor rubbed his stomach with one hand.

"Are you crazy? I'll vomit if I eat anything right now." Sarah
shook her head. "I think I'll just go sit down and wait for you."
She pointed to the bench by the tree."

Taylor shrugged his shoulders and headed off to find him
something to eat. Sarah walked slowly over to the bench and sat
down. She hoped that a little rest would help her to get her
bearings and stop the churning in her stomach. Leaning forward,
she closed her eyes and rested her face in her hands.

"Why are you still here?"

The voice came from behind her. Sarah sat up straight and
swung around to face him. He was kneeling behind the bench
with his arms resting on the back of it.

Dumbfounded, Sarah couldn't think of a single thing to say.
All she could do was stare at him.

He smiled. "Do you like the Ferris wheel?"

She nodded, still unable to find her voice.

"We should ride it then." He stepped around the bench and
held out his hand to her. There was something about him that
just seemed to scream at her senses, warning her off, but she
wanted to talk to him, she wanted to be near him. He wore black
clothing and boots, and although the night was warm, he also
wore a long black coat.

"I'm waiting for my friend," she told him, trying to look
away.

He kneeled down in front of the bench and shook his head.
"You have been waiting for me Sarah."

Was he right? Had she been secretly hoping that it had not
been her imagination, and that he would make another
appearance?

She started to shake her head in denial, but he held up a
hand to stop her. "Sarah … you can't lie to me."

His eyes locked with hers, and he seemed to be staring right
into her soul, peeling back the layers of who she was, until the
person that was Sarah Fabre was naked and vulnerable. She
blinked rapidly, trying to direct her gaze somewhere else, but she
couldn't.

"What's your name?" she forced her vocal cords to work.

"If I tell you my name, will you go on a ride with me?"

"Maybe," Sarah told him.

A smile touched his lips. "My name is Darrien."

"Taylor did a banishing spell on you. How come you are here?"

"Why would he do that? Are you still frightened of me?" A hard glint formed in his dark eyes.

"You were outside the truck window while we were driving," she accused. "You nearly caused us to wreck."

"I'm afraid that you must be mistaken."

Sarah shook her head. "I saw you."

Darrien watched her as if he were trying to uncover some deception in her words. "Well it was not me," he assured her.

Sarah opened her mouth to insist that it was him that she'd seen, but she was starting to doubt it herself. It had not actually been a full-bodied person, but more of an apparition that had appeared outside of the truck's window.

"So will you ride with me?" he asked again.

Sarah took the hand that he held out to her. His touch was cool, and somehow familiar.

Holding her hand, Darrien led her to the large Ferris wheel. It was not one of the most popular rides, so they did not have to wait long before it was their turn. Soon they were in their seat and rising above the lights.

"Why did you want me to ride with you?" she asked.

He smiled. "I wanted to talk with you without being overheard, but in a place that you would feel safe."

"You could kill me up here and be gone before anyone even knew what had happened. I'm really not that dumb. I come from a family of very powerful witches," she told him, hoping to deter any thoughts he might have of carrying out his earlier attempt on her life.

His laughter was dark, but not really threatening. "Yes, I'm aware of that. The Coven of Lazar ... progeny of the dark prince himself."

"What is that suppose to mean?" she asked, narrowing her eyes to glare at him.

"You don't know the stories of the Coven of Lazar and the Fabre witches?" he mocked her.

"I know nothing of a dark prince." Sarah continued to glare at him.

"What a shame. This talk we need to have would be so much easier if you were not ignorant of your beginnings."

"Why don't you just tell me what's going on and why someone wanted you to kill me?" Sarah's temper was starting to get the best of her, and his nearness was making her a little uncomfortable.

The intensity of his eyes and the way the wind tugged at the silky strands of his hair, made for a compelling picture. Sarah had to fight the sudden urge to reach up and run her fingers through that hair.

As if aware of her thoughts, a smile touched his lips. "Are you a virgin Sarah?"

Shocked, Sarah's mouth dropped open. "That's not your business," she told him, her face reddening. The initial shock that she felt was quickly replaced with embarrassment.

Of course she was no virgin. How did you get through two years of college without some experience? Remaining a virgin would be impossible for the lusty Fabre women, at least according to everything she knew about her family history. But she didn't exactly have a lot of experience either.

"Let's find out." Darrien pulled her closer to him, and touched her lips with his. Though she knew she should pull away, Sarah couldn't make herself do it. She was quickly lost in the sensation of his tongue invading her mouth, and his hand caressing the skin on her neck. But there was something else. She could feel his soul burning with the hunger, and a need to consume her - to take in every ounce of her body and spirit.

Sarah was breathless when he finally pulled away.

"You are no virgin. Your hunger for the flesh is almost as strong as mine." His smile was dark and sadistic, but not like it had been only a short time ago. Darrien seemed to have lost some of that black poison that she had sensed permeating his mind.

Sarah tried to block out what she was feeling, how his kiss had taken control of her senses. She couldn't let herself get caught up in him. He was a vampire, a creature of myth, and of death.

She had to force herself to say something, anything to break the spell of the moment. "You still have not answered my question. Why did you come here to kill me?"

Darrien grabbed a handful of her long red hair and gently wrapped it around his fingers, caressing it as if he just couldn't get enough of how it felt against his skin.

He didn't answer her. Instead, he closed his eyes. It was like he could not bear to look at her any longer. She waited for him to respond, but when he again opened his eyes, they were ravenous with hunger, and his lips claimed hers again.

While her mind was screaming at her to push him away, her heart was fluttering as if she had butterflies in her chest. She returned his kiss, leaning up against him so that she could feel even more of him. He broke the kiss just long enough to bite at her bottom lip, sucking at the tiny drops of blood that flowed from her pierced flesh.

The sensation was too intense for her to feel any fear. Sarah bit at his flesh, a sudden craving for his blood spread through her body until she felt as if she would burn up. He abruptly pushed her away.

"Do not taste my blood Sarah," he told her softly.

"Why not?" The hunger was still burning within her, and she tried to grab his lips with her teeth.

Darrien's hands were on her shoulders, and he shook her gently. "Sarah stop!"

Sarah found herself brought back to the moment so quickly it felt like she'd been dropped from the sky to land roughly on the ground. She blinked, trying to remember where she was.

The ride had stopped and the attendant was looking at them as if he'd caught them doing something that they shouldn't have been doing in such a public place.

Darrien helped her off the ride and led her away from the crowd. Sarah looked up and saw Taylor glaring at them angrily. She was ridden with guilt at the realization that she'd completely forgotten about her friend.

Taylor walked over to them, taking slow - cautious steps. As he made his way closer, Sarah could hear that he was chanting something under his breath.

"I'm sorry Taylor. I didn't think the ride would take so long," Sarah apologized.

Taylor scowled, his eyes throwing daggers at Darrien. "I banished you! What are you doing here?"

The darkness that she had sensed in Darrien was back instantly. "No you didn't," he told Taylor.

"Yes I did!"

"No you didn't." Darrien gave him a malicious smile.

Taylor's hand shot out to grab Sarah's arm, and he quickly pulled her away from Darrien. "We need to go," he told her, his voice shaking with urgency.

Taylor tried to lead her away, but Sarah stopped and turned back to Darrien. He was still watching, but it didn't appear that he would try and stop them from leaving.

"You never answered my question," she called out to him.

Darrien gave her one of his dark - haunting smiles. "I will come and visit you again Sarah," he answered, loud enough that she could hear him over the carnival music.

"No you won't!" Taylor yelled back at Darrien. "I'll put you back in the grave where you belong!"

Sarah pulled away from him roughly. "Really Taylor! You have no manners at all."

"Manners!" He was incredulous. "Have you gone crazy Sarah? He is a vampire! What part of that are you not getting?"

"I know what he is," she shot back.

"And?"

After taking a moment to think about it, Sarah realized that she didn't understand why she'd gone off with Darrien, or why she was so attracted to him. "And I don't know," she said, shrugging her shoulders.

"Did you know that the vampire's spell over the opposite sex is more powerful than even the witch's spell?" he asked.

"No I didn't," Sarah admitted. The truth was she didn't know that much about vampires at all, outside of what was in movies and books. She'd been striving so hard to be normal that she had ignored her heritage, and any knowledge she might have gained from the coven.

"How did you know he was a vampire?" she asked.

"If you didn't notice, he has almost no color, and he has a darkness about him that you can feel as soon as you look at him."

"Why didn't you feel it in the truck then?"

He paused, as if he was unsure himself. "I don't know. Maybe what you saw was not a vampire?" Taylor started walking toward the exit. "That might explain why the banishing spell didn't work."

"What could it have been then?"

"Maybe a warning," Taylor told her, a cryptic note in his voice.

"Why are we going already?" she wanted to know.

"We need to talk with your aunt and tell her about this," he said, looking over his shoulder at her.

Sighing, Sarah followed him out the exit gate. "I think you are taking all of this a little too seriously. Besides, Aunt Jeanie already knows about him."

"Damn it Sarah!" he yelled. "I was responsible for you tonight. You should have told me where you were going."

Sarah was shocked. Taylor had never raised his voice to her before. "I'm sorry. I really didn't think it was a big deal."

Taylor grumbled something under his breath, but said no more on the subject.

Sarah stopped and looked back at the carnival. She wondered where Darrien was at that moment.

Was he still watching her?

Why was he the only thing that she could think of? Had he looked into her eyes, and cast some type of spell on her that had taken control of her mind and body? Sarah closed her eyes and tried to forget how she'd felt when he'd kissed her.

It was no use. His presence was as strong as if he were still standing beside her. Sarah turned away from the carnival lights to see that Taylor was standing by the truck, waiting for her.

She could not hold it against Taylor. He was concerned about her, that's all. Sarah continued to the truck and got in. She smiled at her friend.

"I really am sorry that I worried you," she told him. "But I don't regret spending a few minutes with him. He's different."

Taylor frowned. "Yeah he's different all right. He's a freaking vampire!"

* * * *

Darrien watched the young man drag Sarah away and a dark shadow of fury descended on him, but he pushed it away. His anger would do little to convince her of the truth, and her need to get away from Sutter Point.

When she'd been in his arms on the beach, bravely facing death, he'd felt compelled to kiss her - to love her. He saw Caroline in her face that night, but he hadn't been sure she was Caroline, not until tonight when he'd once again held her in his arms. The connection was still there. She was his beloved Caroline, the woman that had ripped apart his soul and left it open for the darkness to consume him.

Caroline had returned to him, just as she had promised. But he'd been sent by an ancient to kill her. Darrien would not do it. He would not be responsible for her death again. This time he would save her, even if she again refused immortality.

He had tried to give Caroline life, but she would not take his blood. Now that Caroline was Sarah, she had wanted his blood. She'd wanted his blood with a hunger so great that he had nearly been taken away by her erotic - all consuming need. This time he would not offer her immortality, but instead he would give her the blessing of being free of his love. She did not need to know the pain of loving an immortal, not again.

He would see that she was safe and then he would return to the darkness that had become so much a part of who he was. But could he hold that darkness at bay long enough to do what was right this time, or would his hunger for her be too much?

Chapter Four

The Lafayette Cemetery was beautiful beneath the early morning sun. Bending down, Nicole lifted the jug of water and poured some of it into the brass container that was attached to the base of the Trenton family tomb. When it was half-full, she took the blue and white daises, and arranged them in the vase until they were exactly the way she wanted them.

Though it had taken a long time, she could now smile when she remembered Jay. His memory could still bring on the tears, but now they were less frequent. She tried to remember the joy her little brother had given her, and not just the sadness of his loss.

If it had not been for Alec, Nicole's grief would have eventually drove her into an abyss of darkness. How ironic that a creature of darkness would be the one to bring new light into her life.

Nicole was worried sick about Alec. He had been gone for days now, and there had still been no word from him.

"Such a tragic loss."

Nicole was startled by the unfamiliar voice.

The man stood only a few feet away. His approach had been so silent that she hadn't a clue someone had been watching her. The stranger's dark eyes were not unsympathetic, but he seemed guarded. He was an older gentleman. Nicole guessed that he was probably in his mid fifties by the lines on his face and the white streaks of gray in his black hair.

"I'm sorry. Do I know you?" Nicole asked.

He shook his head. "I'm afraid that I've never had the pleasure. My name is Lex," he told her.

Nicole got to her feet. Though she didn't flee from the stranger, she was cautious. She'd grown so accustomed to being on the lookout for Omar's vamps, that she now treated all strangers with suspicion.

"Hello," she gave him a nod.

"I am an acquaintance of your friend Ethan," he explained.

"Oh, are you the …"

"The lycan," he finished for her. "Yes that is what I am. My pack is known as the *Vilka*."

"What information do you have about my sisters?" Nicole asked. She had wanted to meet Ethan's mysterious informant for some time now. She wanted the opportunity question him herself.

"Do you mind?" he asked, motioning to a bench near the Trenton family tomb.

"No … not at all."

"Please sit with me a while." He patted the space next to him on the bench.

Nicole hesitated only a moment before deciding that he was not a threat, and sat down beside him. Although she was a born vampire that could live in the light, and without blood for nourishment, she still had some of the instincts of the vampire. Wariness of the lycan was one of the instincts bred into her.

"Your little brother." Lex pointed toward the tomb. "He died from an accidental drowning, as I understand."

Nicole nodded. "Yes. He suffered a fever induced seizure while he was in the tub."

"I'm sorry to hear that. It is always sad when a young child dies."

She felt genuine sympathy from the man. Nicole decided that she really liked the lycan.

"Thank you. Dealing with his death has been very difficult."

"Yes, I'm sure it has."

"What about my sisters? What do you know about them?" Nicole reminded him of her question of a few moments before.

Lex studied her face for a long time before answering. "I know the location of one of them, but I am not sure about the other."

Nicole waited for him to continue, but he said no more.

"Well," she prodded him for more information.

"My adopted granddaughter is your sister, but I cannot reveal anything about her at this time. It is too dangerous."

"The sooner we find both of them, the sooner we can stop Omar and his followers," she reasoned.

"This is true," he agreed. "But she has not reached the point that she is ready. To expose her now could be disastrous for all three of you. The one that you need to worry about is still out there somewhere, and probably unprotected."

"What can you tell me about the other one then?" Nicole asked.

"I can tell you that she is descended from a line of very powerful witches … the Fabre witches. You may have heard of them. They are legend in New Orleans. Some say that Marie Laveau was the illegitimate daughter of one of the Fabre men."

Nicole was ready to tell him that she did not believe in witches, but then she knew just how ridiculous that would sound. Her lover was a vampire, and here she was talking to a lycan.

"So if we can trace the descendants of these witches, then we might be able to find her?" Nicole asked.

Lex nodded. "I don't believe they are in this area any longer. They were run out of here a long time ago."

"Well if they were all that notorious, they shouldn't be too difficult to track down."

"That's true, but it is true for Omar as well. She could be in grave danger." Lex gazed at the tomb. "You would not want to lose another sibling."

"Why doesn't my father know more?"

Lex gave her a cynical smile. "Your father does know more than what he is telling you. To help you out too much would be going against his own species. Have you thought of that?"

"Yes, but we are his children?"

Lex nodded. "I suspect that is the reason he wants you to find your sisters. He wants his children protected, but he cannot be the one to go against the vampires."

"What about the Place of Light? You come from there … don't you?" Nicole asked, though she already knew that he did.

"Yes, but I have been banished from that place."

Nicole wanted to ask why, but thought it would be too impolite.

Sensing her curiosity, Lex volunteered the information. "I was the leader of an extremely powerful warrior society, but I let my hate and bigotry consume the person that I was. It almost cost me my daughter."

"And they banished you?"

"Yes, until such time that I have redeemed myself," he smiled sadly.

"This is why you wish to help the vampires?" Nicole was trying to put the pieces together.

"My granddaughter … she is very important to me. I feel without intervention that all three of you may perish."

This wasn't exactly what Nicole had hoped to hear. "Why can't the vampires go to this Place of Light?"

"This is your history … not mine. It isn't my place to tell you about matters that the elders of your race don't wish you to know."

"But you admit that knowledge of this place would help bring down Omar's plan of domination."

"Yes, if the vampires knew of this place, it would take away a lot of Omar's power. But this place doesn't have much to do with what the vampire is, or the truth of their origins. This knowledge is really very sensitive, and could be dangerous for the immortals, as well as humans. The ancients must release this information carefully. I suspect this is why your father has not told you more."

"Can I go to this Place of Light, or am I also forbidden?"

"Humans are generally forbidden, with only a few exceptions. There is only one vampire there. It is this vampire that educated us on the immortal."

"So the people that live in this place only know what they were taught by this vampire?"

Lex nodded. "He is an ancient, like your father and Omar."

"Why is he there?"

"Again ... I cannot give you that information, because it has to do with the history of the immortals"

"But if I ever do go there ... I can contact my little brother again?" she asked, hopefully.

Lex smiled. "I see that someone has been giving away the secrets of *Outerlands*." He stood and held out a hand to help her to her feet. "Yes there is a way, if you can get into *Outerlands*. But there is much work to be done before this would ever be a possibility."

"I don't understand."

"The wolves and the immortals have been enemies for a very long time. There must be some kind of harmony between them before the vampire would be permitted entrance into that dimension of reality. The wolves are the protectors of the earth ... the vampires have no regard for life."

"They are hunters the same as the wolves." Nicole felt compelled to defend her father's species.

"This is true. The wolves do hunt, but they hunt to feed and not just to kill. The immortals have evolved into a species that feeds off of the darkness and the fear in men's souls, and not just their blood. Blood is easy to come by without having to slaughter. Ask your friend Dash. He received a gift from the *Outerlands* ... a recipe."

"Dash's recipe?" Nicole was stunned. It had come from the Place of Light. They were trying to help the vampires.

"You must go now, and do what you can to find your sister," Lex told her.

"Where can I find you if I need to talk with you again?"

"I will find you," he promised.

Chapter Five

Sarah dried the last plate and placed it in the cupboard on top of a large stack of identical plates. She had volunteered to cleanup after dinner. Jeanie was having one of her bad days, as she called them. Her feet were swollen to twice their usual size, and it was difficult for her to stand on them for too long.

Sarah feared that it was a sign of heart disease, but Jeanie would not go to the town doctor. She insisted that it was nothing that a strong spell and some good old fashion rest, wouldn't fix.

Aunt Jeanie hadn't been nearly as upset as Sarah had thought she'd be, when Taylor brought her home, and spilled the beans about Darrien. Jeanie had given Sarah a look of disapproval, and then told them that she would prefer to discuss the situation after the summer solstice.

Sarah was almost looking forward to the Midsummer's Eve celebration, just so she could find out some of the secrets she was sure Jeanie was keeping from her. Just as Sarah finished cleaning the sink and hanging the dishtowel, she heard the doorbell.

"I'll get it," Jeanie called from the parlor where she had been reading one of the latest novels from her favorite author.

A moment later Jeanie walked into the kitchen, her face as pale as death. "He's here," she whispered.

It had to be Darrien.

Sarah wanted to rush to the front door, but instead she forced a casual pace as she went to greet him.

Darrien nodded to her. "Sarah."

"Hi,' she smiled.

"Would you walk on the beach with me so we can finish our talk?" he asked.

"I don't think so," Aunt Jeanie broke in.

"It's okay," Sarah assured her.

"No it is not okay." Jeanie was glaring at Darrien.

"Madam … it is vital that I speak with Sarah in private. I will not hurt her," he promised.

"I'll be right back," Sarah put in before her aunt could protest further.

Jeanie shook her head. "You should at least wait until after the solstice. It is only a few more days away."

Sarah shook her head. "Don't worry," she told her aunt.

Aunt Sarah went to a cabinet and quickly rummaged through it. Finally she pulled out a long chain with a blue crystal. "Wear this," she said, handing the necklace to Sarah. "That way I can feel it if you are in trouble."

Sarah placed the silver chain around her neck so that Jeanie wouldn't fret so much about her being with Darrien. Jeanie had an identical crystal around her neck. Sarah knew that these crystals would make the psychic connection between them stronger.

"I'll be back soon," Sarah told Jeanie, kissing her on the cheek before leaving.

"Your aunt is very protective," he commented when they were outside the house.

"She doesn't like vampires."

"Yes, I gathered that much."

The two of them took the path down the hillside to the beach. When they reached the bottom, Darrien took her hand in his and pulled her to the sand. Beneath the bright moonlight, he appeared ethereal - even magical. Looking at him at that moment, Sarah wondered if she was dreaming. Never had she been in the presence of a man so perfect - so male.

It had to be the vampire's spell.

Sarah grasped at something that would keep her anchored to reality. "What did you want to talk with me about?"

Darrien squeezed her hand softly. "Sarah … you are in danger. You must go into hiding."

"You keep telling me this, but you won't give me any details."

"Omar is the leader of a very old and powerful tribe of vampires, and he wants you dead," he told her.

"Why would he bother with me? I'm just a human. A witch that does not even practice the craft." Sarah could not understand why all of this was happening to her. She was nobody really.

"You are his niece, and one of three sisters that will bring an end to the rule of the ancients. At least this is what Omar believes," he explained.

Sarah shook her head. "You must be mistaken. I have no sisters."

Darrien smiled patiently. "But you do Sarah."

"My father died when I was a baby. That's what my mother told me." Sarah looked away. She had never known her father, and truthfully hadn't thought a lot about the man that had sired her. He'd never been a part of her life, and he just didn't seem real to her.

Darrien reached up to brush a strand of hair away from her eyes. "Your mother did not tell you the truth."

"What do you mean?" Sarah frowned.

"Your father is a vampire Sarah, as you are as well."

Sarah laughed. "I know you have the wrong girl now. I have no problem with sunlight, and I don't need blood."

"Don't you?" Darrien arched one brow. "You became intoxicated by the scent of my blood."

Sarah's face reddened and she was glad for the cover of darkness. The urge to consume his blood had stripped her of all capacity to reason. Even now, the very thought of tasting him - of taking his blood into her mouth, left her feeling dizzy with hunger. The hunger was so erotic that it obscured her ability to think.

"I see that the urge has not left you," Darrien laughed.

"But I can be in the light," she insisted.

"Yes, a gift from your human mother."

"Is this why you said I was descended from the dark prince?"

Darrien shook his head. "No, that is a legend exclusive to the Fabre witches. They are known as the daughters of darkness that descended from Satan himself. But I believe this to be just legend. They are powerful witches, and power breeds jealousy, which of course leads to rumors."

"But you didn't kill me ... why?"

Darrien gazed at her for a long time, his eyes working their magic on her senses, until Sarah felt as if he was all that existed for her. Without answering her, he leaned over and kissed her lips softly.

Sarah lost herself in the pure sensation of his lips on hers, and the way it felt to have his tongue exploring her mouth. Touching his hair, she relished the feeling of the silky strands between her fingers. She just could not get enough of him, of the way he touched her, the way it made her feel to look into his eyes. She found it strangely erotic to know that to be close to him, was to be close to death. The danger only made her crave his touch all the more.

Darrien pulled away so that she could breathe. His hand came up to caress her cheek. "I cannot kill you Sarah. It is because of me that you died once. I will not be responsible for it again."

Sarah shook her head, completely confused by his words. "I'm lost. What do you mean I died once?"

"You have powers beyond most of the other Lazar witches, don't you?"

Sarah shrugged her shoulders. "I don't know. Aunt Jeanie says so."

"That is because you lived before. I didn't realize who you were until I kissed you the first time," he confessed. "Even then, I thought it was too good to be true. I could not believe that you had really come back to me."

"Who is it that you are talking about?" Sarah was hurt that he was thinking of someone else - thinking that she was someone else.

"Caroline Fabre. She was your ancestress," Darrien told her as he continued to caress her skin with his fingers.

Sarah pushed his hand away. "No, I am Sarah. Not this Caroline that you seem to want me to be."

Darrien smiled. "Don't be jealous Sarah. You and Caroline are one in the same."

"Don't be ridiculous! I'm not jealous," Sarah scowled. "I just don't want to be thought of as someone else."

Without saying anything, Darrien kissed her. Sarah tried to resist - tried to force herself to remember that it was the ghost of another woman that he wanted. When he looked at her, it was someone else that he was seeing.

It was no use. As soon as he pulled her close and his mouth was on hers, all that she could think about was being in his arms. She wanted more. Sarah wanted his hands touching her everywhere, to feel his teeth in her flesh, as her warm blood flowed from her body.

His lips moved to her throat, she could feel his teeth on her skin, and the sensation was driving her insane. His hands slipped beneath her blouse and he freed her breasts from the confines of her bra. The coolness of his touch against her warm breasts was tantalizing. Sarah gasped, as he gently squeezed and pulled at her budding nipples.

"Feed on me," she breathed.

Darrien froze. "You do not want that Sarah," he whispered.

"Oh … I *do* want that," she moaned.

"You are a born vampire Sarah. You could be easily infected, and then you would be like me," he told her.

Sarah tried to get her breathing under control. Her need for him was so intense that she felt compelled to consume him. She wanted to feel him within her, feeding her need with his desire. She wanted to taste him, as he was taking her to that ultimate paradise. The thought made her tremble.

Sarah forced herself to remember that what she was feeling was really the vampire's spell.

Swallowing hard, Sarah pulled away from him. "I don't know what to think of all of this."

"Search inside of yourself Sarah, and you will find that what I am telling you is true. You are Caroline." He tried to pull her close, but she resisted.

"And the born vampire thing ... what about that?" she asked. Sarah's mind was reeling. All of this just seemed to be too much.

"I suspect that you can verify this with your aunt."

"And the reason that you care what happens to me is because you think I am this dead witch?" Sarah eyes strayed toward the sea. She couldn't let herself look at him or she would be lost. As soon as she looked into his eyes, she wouldn't care about anything but being with him. Something told her that she needed to stay in control right now.

"That is one reason, yes."

"What is it that you want from me? Do you want me to pretend that I am this witch?"

Darrien shook his head. "I just do not want to be responsible for your demise. This is why I want you to go away before Omar sends someone else to kill you. It is also why I must not come to you again," he added in a soft voice.

Sarah turned sharply to face him. The thought of never seeing him again was troubling. "So is that what this was about? You've come to tell me this, and then you plan to go away?"

Darrien nodded. For a moment it appeared that he was going to say something more, but he didn't.

Sarah turned away. "Well I'm not running!

"Don't be foolish Sarah! These are immortals. They cannot die, at least not by any normal means. For you to do battle with them, would be asking for death." Darrien's voice shook with frustration and anger.

"I will be initiated at the summer solstice, and then the coven will stand with me," she told him, a stubborn glint in her eyes.

Darrien jumped to his feet. "If you will not help yourself Sarah, there is nothing more that I can do for you."

"How do you suppose that I help myself, go hide in a hole for the rest of my life? If there is any truth to what you tell me, maybe I should be looking for these sisters and doing what it is we are supposed to do?" Sarah snapped.

"The sisters have no chance of success. The ancients are too powerful."

Sarah stood and took his hand in hers. "Darrien, stay with me and help me."

He refused to look at her. "I cannot do that. The last time I was a part of your life …" his voice trailed off and he became silent.

Sarah drew her brows together. "I don't believe that I am this witch that you say I am."

"You are wrong," he shook his head. "Once two souls have come together in love, as we did, they are connected throughout eternity. Search inside yourself, and you will find that connection."

Sarah could not deny that there was something there. Though she had no conscious memory of Darrien before she'd seen him standing out in her aunt's garden that night, she did feel as if she knew him.

"If this is true, why are you planning to go away?" she asked, her heart sinking at the very thought of never seeing him again.

Finally he let his eyes rest on her face. "I will only end up hurting you Sarah. It is what happened before. Your death was my fault."

"How was it your fault?" Sarah was becoming aggravated with him.

Darrien shook his head. "There is no time for all of this. Even right now, Omar is wondering where I am. He will send someone else soon."

Sarah let go of his hand. "Then go! I will fight these vampires, and I *will* win."

Darrien's anger erupted. "Do you think you could fight against an immortal?" he growled. His anger shone through his eyes, and she saw him transform into something dark and deadly. Snarling, he drew back his teeth to reveal fangs. His hand whipped out to grasp her arm.

Sarah tried to pull away, her heart pounding with fear. He held her arm tightly, forcing her into the sand. "Do you think you could stop me, if I wanted to kill you?" His fury made his voice sound deep and guttural. In that instant, he resembling something far from human.

He was lying on top of her, his body pinning her down so that she could not move. "Do you want to know what it is like to be fed on by an immortal?" he roared.

Lifting her shirt, he stared down at her heaving chest and naked breasts. Sarah gasped when she felt his wet tongue sliding over her taut nipples. Then she felt the pressure of his fangs on her flesh, and the sensation of warm blood spilling across her breast. Fire erupted between her legs, and she let out a soft moan, lifting her chest to feed him more.

She could feel his stiff desire pressing hard against her stomach, and she wiggled beneath him, so that she could feel him better. Her actions fanned the flames of his hunger, and he pulled away from her. Throwing his head back, he roared in frustration. He swiftly got to his feet, as if her nearness was too unbearable to endure any longer.

"Cover yourself," he told her, his voice so low that she had to strain to hear him.

Pulling her shirt down, Sarah stood up. "Why do you keep pushing me away? I can tell that you want it too."

"Yes, I want you," he admitted. "I want you so much that I could easily lose control and take your life, or turn you."

"You are angry because you couldn't scare me like you were trying to do," Sarah accused.

Darrien shook his head. "Sarah … your hunger will control you one day, if you do not take control of it now. If you were someone else, this would have frightened you, but it only made your craving worse."

Sarah stepped closer and rested her hand on his arm. "I don't want you to go away."

Darrien glanced at her. "I can't be close to you … and not touch you."

"I want you to," she insisted.

He shook his head. "I can't."

"I am not that person. I am not Caroline," Sarah told him angrily.

"Go to your coven Sarah and ask for their protection. I cannot protect you, not even from me." Darrien took her hand in his and started walking back to the house.

"Where will you go?" she asked.

"It doesn't matter. One place is the same as the next for me."

Sarah stopped suddenly. "You still haven't told me anything about who you are, just your name."

He stared at her, his dark eyes reflecting the silver moonlight. She wanted so badly to reach out and touch him, but she feared his rejection. It was far more painful than when his teeth punctured her flesh.

"I am death. That's all you need to know about me," he told her before turning away and starting up the path to her aunt's house.

"But what if I remember … from that other life. What if I come looking for you?" she was desperate to get anything from him that would help her find him again.

"You don't know how badly I want you to remember me, but perhaps it is best that you don't."

They had reached the front porch and he dropped her hand. Darrien leaned down and brushed her lips with his. "Stay out of the dark," he told her. "And be careful who you trust."

A lump formed in her throat as she watched him retreat into the darkness. Sarah felt anger mixed with her sadness.

Chapter Six

Peering through the thick darkness, Alec made his way along the passages beneath Castle Arges. All that could be heard was a slow - steady dripping of water, the result of condensation on the rock walls. Originally, the hidden passages beneath the castle had been used as an escape route. Just incase the family in residence should come under attack. The passages connected to different areas of the castle, and to tunnels that led to the village at the bottom of the cliff. This was common knowledge, but Alec discovered there were also hidden passages.

Luciano had occupied the castle for the past two centuries. He rarely left the safety of his haven, and shunned all that sought an audience with him, even the ancients. Secrecy among the oldest vampires was not unusual, but Luciano took it far beyond the norm. But considering his reputation, it was no small wonder that he kept to himself. It was a widespread theory among vampires and slayers, that if you could destroy Luciano, you would break the curse of the immortal, but Alec wasn't convinced.

The passages beneath the castle seemed to go on forever. Alec had no idea where he would find the Book of Anu. If the manuscript was in the castle, it was hidden well. Donavan had hinted to a relic that was held in Luciano's possession. The manuscript was the most legendary of the vampire relics, so it had to be what Luciano was hiding.

About a hundred feet ahead of him, the passage took a sharp curve to the left. Flickering light pierced the heavy darkness, it was the only light that Alec had seen since entering the passageway. Staying close to the rock wall, Alec moved cautiously toward the light. When he reached the area where the tunnel curved, he peeked around the wall. The light was coming from torches that stood on each side of a large doorway.

He moved quickly to the door. Keeping close to the wall, Alec peered inside. It appeared to be some type of chamber. Unlike the rest of the subterranean rooms, the walls in this chamber were smooth, and adorned with strange symbols painted in metallic gold. Two more torches illuminated another doorway at the far end of the chamber.

Entering cautiously, he moved toward the second doorway. Unlike the first chamber, a metal door blocked his entrance to whatever lay beyond. Alec pulled on the handle and the door opened easily. Behind the door was another tunnel, this one descending deeper into the earth.

Alec stepped into the darkness, but froze when her heard the deep laughter behind him. He looked back to see Luciano watching him, a look of amusement on his face.

"It has been a long time since you tried to infiltrate my home. Whatever it is that you are looking for, you won't find it in that tunnel."

Alec turned to face Luciano. "Where does the passage go?"

Luciano scrutinized him, his black eyes stabbing painfully into Alec's brain. Being in the ancient vampire's presence was so overwhelming that it was like being in the throes of death - blissful but painful. The vampire's long black hair was immaculately kept, and his soft features were too perfect to ever have been human. But his perfection was marred by the darkness that ate at his soul.

"It leads nowhere, at least for you," Luciano told him.

"What is it that you are hiding down there Luciano?" Alec asked him. He was already in danger, pushing for an answer was not likely to cause him any further peril.

Again Alec felt shattering pain behind his eyes, as Luciano probed his mind. It lasted only a few seconds, before he heard the vampire's voice break through the agony in his head.

"What you seek is not down there." Luciano stepped closer and leaned down to whisper in Alec's ear. "The Book of Anu is not here, it is not even in Romania."

"If it is not down there, what is it that is at the end of these passages?" Alec questioned him, no longer caring what it might cost him.

"You will live an eternity Alec, and still it will not be long enough for you to discover what is at the end of that passageway." Luciano taunted.

"What do you plan to do with me?" Alec got straight to the point. He had no intention of playing a game of words with Luciano.

Luciano smiled. "Alec, you place far too much importance on yourself. I would not have even interrupted your invasion of my home, if not for the fact that I find you amusing … a break from the monotony."

"Where can I find the book Luciano? The rule of the ancients is coming to an end. The Light Seeker movement will spread, and then there will be trouble for all of you."

Luciano waved his hand, indicating that Alec's words were of no consequence. "You must have a desire to rule before the threat of the Light Seekers is relevant. It may matter to Omar, but I do not care to have power over others. I want only to be left alone."

Alec shook his head. "Why?"

Luciano's dark eyes became like stones. "When and if you ever find the Book of Anu, you will find out why ruling over the mutant vampires means little to me."

"Where do I find this book?" Alec decided to push his advantage. At least Luciano was talking, and that was further than he'd ever gotten with the vampire before.

The hardness left the vampire's eyes to be replaced by humor. "You are on a fool's mission Alec," Luciano smiled. "But if you insist on finding those elusive answers that you seek ... you will want to search in Rome. I hear that the holy men of the Vatican are keeping it under lock and key."

"So it does exist?" Alec asked.

Again Luciano shrugged his shoulders. "It is believed that a rebel recorded our history in this manuscript, but I cannot tell you if it *still* exists."

"Don't you realize what could happen if Omar follows through with this plan to dominate all vampires? Already his followers feed off of the fear they inspire in the mortals. They do not treat them as a necessity, but as a feast."

"Omar is a fool and will perish because of it. His brothers must intervene ... it is not my concern."

"But you are the most powerful of the ancients. It would be easy for you to stop him," Alec insisted, boldly stepping toward Luciano.

"Neither species is worth the trouble," Luciano glared at Alec. "Now be on your way. I have grown tired of this exchange of meaningless words."

"Maybe you are a coward and are afraid to go against Omar?" Alec knew his words were a mistake, but he could not take them back, and wouldn't have, even if he could.

An unnatural light entered Luciano's eyes. It was the only sign of his rage. "You will remove yourself from my sight Alec Norwood, or you will die with Omar."

Alec's own rage gripped him and he wanted to fly toward Luciano and tear the vampire to pieces. What right did these ancients have to keep the truth hidden from their own kind?

It took every ounce of control to keep from going with his instincts. He would not survive a fight with Luciano. No vampire in existence would. Luciano's mind was so powerful, that he could pierce the heart and brain, and bleed his victims to death, without ever physically touching them. He was just as deadly to the vampires as he was the human race, maybe more so.

* * * *

The fading sun cast the forest deep in shadow. Sarah followed her aunt down the narrow path to the large clearing. For almost a hundred years, the Coven of Lazar had gathered for their celebrations and Sabbaths in the woods near Sutter Point. The area was surrounded with thick pines and foliage. It would not be easy to find, unless you knew where to look.

Sarah lifted the hem of her robe to keep it from catching on low-lying branches and rocks. Though she had been fighting against the idea of being initiated into the coven, she found her excitement growing. After all, the coven was her heritage and a part of who she was.

The scent of burning wood filled the air. In the clearing a large bonfire burned, and dozens of people in bright colored robes of yellow, blue and green milled around, preparing for the night's festivities. Sarah's robe was black, the color of the initiate. Once she had gone through the rites, she would then wear a robe of another color.

The Coven of Lazar consisted of nearly fifty members, but many of them lived nowhere near Sutter Point. Coven members would travel from all over the country to attend the Sabbaths in Sutter Point.

Jeanie carried a large bowl of cakes that would be included in the feast once the ceremonies were done. She handed the bowl off to another member of the coven, and grabbed Sarah's hand. The two of them followed another path to a smaller clearing, where Sarah would wait until it was time for the initiation rites.

Aunt Jeanie pointed to the bench. "You can wait here. Someone will come and get you when it's time."

Sarah sat on the bench. Being the only initiate, she would remain in the clearing alone, until it was time for her to join the rest of the coven. Someone had lit a small fire near the bench, so she wouldn't be left in total darkness once the sun was down.

The forest beyond the clearing was already murky. Sarah peered into that darkness, hoping that Darrien was out there waiting for night - waiting for the moment that he could come to her. With a deep sigh, Sarah pushed the thought away. She had not seen him since that night on the beach. He must have gone away like he'd told her he would.

Her eyes strayed to the shadows that were gathering in the woods. She could not help but wonder if there was someone else out there - someone that would be a lot more dangerous than Darrien. Though anything was possible, Sarah doubted any vampire would dare attack her with the coven so close. One witch may not be so difficult to deal with, but an entire coven was another matter.

Since Darrien's revelations about her past and who she was, Sarah's mind had been in a whirlwind. Whoever Darrien was, she felt a connection with him that she had never felt with anyone else. Now that he was gone, it was as if an important part of her was missing.

Then there were all of the questions - questions that she just didn't have answers for. Was she really the daughter of a vampire, and the reincarnated spirit of her long dead ancestress?

Once she'd been brought into the coven, Sarah intended to get some answers from her aunt. Maybe she could even find out more about what happened to her mother? The ritual for honoring the summer solstice was now underway, Sarah could hear the members of the coven chanting in the distance. When they had concluded the ritual, someone would come to get her.

Though the ritual for the summer solstice lasted only a short time, to Sarah it felt like hours. Finally Taylor emerged from the darkness and stepped into the clearing. He wore a dark blue robe with a large hood pulled over his head. Without saying a word to her, Taylor covered her eyes with a blindfold and took her by the hand.

Sarah could see nothing, but she sensed when they had come into the larger clearing. She knew that Taylor would lead her to the altar where Aunt Jeanie was waiting for her. Jeanie was the high priestess of the Coven of Lazar, and had been since the day her grandmother had passed into the afterlife.

"Who approaches the sacred altar of the god and goddess?" It was her aunt's voice.

"I bring you one that seeks the wisdom of the coven. I bring you one that will honor the god and goddess," Taylor answered.

"By what name will you be known as a member of the Coven of Lazar?" Jeanie asked.

"Caroline." The name slipped out before she'd even had time to think about what she was saying.

"Enter the sacred circle of the coven and kneel before the gods."

Sarah stepped forward, entering the sacred space that was filled with the presence of the gods, and the spirits of her ancestors. She knelt before the altar.

Aunt Jeanie's voice was distant and far away. The air was hot - so hot that she could not get any oxygen from it. She was gasping, trying to draw in more air, but it was too thin, and too hot to breathe. The world went dark, and then she was somewhere else.

Luis was screaming, calling her name over and over again. Her husband had gone to the barn to check on the animals. They'd been restless all night, and he was worried a wolf was about - just waiting to get to their milking cows and chickens.

She peered down at her shoes, but they were not hers. The brown leather was worn, and she could see her stockings peeking out of the seams. The long skirt was also faded and tattered. She was no longer Sarah, but Caroline.

Rushing from the small farmhouse, she raced to the barn where she could still hear Luis screaming. Just as she reached for the barn door to pull it open, Luis' screams faded and the night was once again silent.

Caroline yanked the door open. What greeted her was more horrifying than anything she could have imagined.

She was a witch, this shouldn't have surprised her, but it did. The mystical creatures known as vampires were something that all witches knew about, but few ever actually encountered them. The form that hovered over her husband, jumped back when she opened the door. He'd retreated into the darkness, out of the reach of the bright moonlight that entered through the open doorway.

Caroline wanted to scream, but she could not utter a sound. The vampire's eyes glowed with his poisonous hunger, and his growls shattered the silent night. The creature flew at her, but she held up her hand and willed all of the power of the universe to surround her, and protect her from his attack.

The vampire seemed to hit a brick wall before he could get close to her. The impact stunned him, and he fell to the ground. When the creature's features returned to normal, Caroline was startled to see a familiar face. The man lying there in the hay was no monster at all, but Lord Rousseau from the chateau near where she'd grownup in France.

What was he doing in New Orleans? What had happened to him to bring him to such a horrible condition?

As a girl, Caroline had been taken with the young man, but he'd barely noticed a poor village girl who was rumored to be the daughter of a witch, at least not at first. Then he did notice her, but soon disappeared. Eventually she had immigrated to the Americas, but over the years she'd never forgotten him. Now here he was, a vampire.

At the moment, he was dazed and not moving. Caroline took the opportunity to go to Luis. When she kneeled next to his pale body, she knew he was gone. The creature had already drained his blood before she could stop him.

Caroline glanced over at the vampire who was beginning to move. When he had recovered enough to sit up, he looked at her and she saw recognition enter his eyes.

"Caroline!"

Caroline said nothing. She continued to watch him, wary that he should make any sudden movements.

He got to his feet and held out a hand to her. Still she didn't move, making no attempt to take the offered hand.

"I'm sorry Caroline. I would not have attacked you ... if I'd been in my right mind."

"You are a creature of evil," she spit out her words.

"Alas you are right, but I won't hurt you Caroline," he smiled darkly.

But he had hurt her, much worse than if he'd taken her life that night.

Sarah came back to the present. She could hear the impatience in her aunt's voice as she repeated her question.

"Are you prepared to begin your life anew?"

"Yes," Sarah answered.

"Rise up from the darkness of yesterday and become one with us."

Sarah rose to her feet and stood still, as two of the female members of the coven untied her robe, and let it slip from her body. She stood before the altar, naked for all to see. This was not something new for the coven, but it made her feel uncomfortable.

Someone was removing the blindfold, and when Sarah opened her eyes, the bright light of the fire sent pain through her head.

"You are born again into the grace of the god and goddess. Receive their protection." Jeanie's voice echoed through the dark forest.

Someone was now placing a white robe over her body. The changing of the robes symbolized her emergence from darkness to light.

Aunt Jeanie stepped from the altar, and carried a small golden dish of burning incense to where Sarah stood. She covered her niece with the purifying smoke of the incense, and when she was done, she stepped back to the altar. The rites of initiation were concluded.

Now they would feast and celebrate throughout the night. Sarah waited patiently for the moment she could get Jeanie alone.

* * * *

The vision of the firelight dancing on the smooth skin of her firm breasts, nearly sent him into a frenzy of hunger. It took all his willpower to keep himself hidden. He could not take his eyes off of her, but at the same time, he felt rage that others were gazing upon her naked flesh.

Darrien knew he should leave and never return, but how could he let her face the fury of Omar alone. He would watch her until the time was right to leave, but he could not let himself get too near her. If he were to make love to her, he would never be able to let her go. In the end, his love would only cause her more suffering.

He closed his eyes so that he would be able to hold his desire at bay. The urge to swoop down and take her away was so great, that he trembled with the effort it took to resist.

Chapter Seven

It was near dawn by the time Sarah and Jeanie returned home. Despite the fact that they were both tired, Sarah wasn't going to bed until she had a chance to talk with her aunt. Jeanie must have already known that sleep wasn't an option yet, because she headed for the kitchen instead of her bedroom.

"Do you want some tea while we talk," Jeanie asked.

Nodding her head, Sarah followed her aunt into the kitchen. Jeanie went about making them both a cup of tea. She waited until Jeanie was done serving them before broaching the questions that she had been dying to ask.

Before Sarah could say anything, Jeanie sat down and turned angry eyes on her. "Did you think I would not notice the bite marks on you?" she asked.

Sarah reddened as she realized how many people had gotten a glimpse of the wounds Darrien had left on her. "To tell you the truth, I didn't think about it at all."

"That is quite clear," Jeanie snapped at her. "What has he done to you? Have you become his feeder?"

Sarah shook her head. "No … things just got out of hand, but it hasn't gone all the way."

"Good, because you need to think about it real hard before you let it go any further," Jeanie told her.

"That vampire, Darrien. He said that my father wasn't dead. That he was a vampire." Sarah changed the subject.

Jeanie's eyes were downcast. "He is telling the truth. I met your father only once. But I can tell you that he was everything that you might think a vampire to be, especially persuasive. Your mother was crazy in love with him."

"What happened to him?"

"He went away. They had a disagreement and he left. She wanted him to change her, but he refused. Told her that you needed a mother."

"So what happened to my mother then?" Sarah asked, afraid that she already knew the answer.

"She went looking for him." Jeanie placed her hand over Sarah's.

"Well what do you think happened to her?"

"I think that she was either killed, or turned by another vampire."

"Why would she do that? She promised to come back for me!" Sarah narrowed her eyes, unable to believe that her mother would really abandon her.

"I know sweetheart. I just don't have the answers." Jeanie squeezed Sarah's hand.

"I should try and find her."

Jeanie shook her head. "I'm sure that if she could have returned, she would have. If you go looking for her, you could be facing the same dangers. I know it isn't something she would want you to do."

"There's something else. Darrien said that he knew me before ... when I was someone else. He said that I was Caroline Fabre."

Jeanie inhaled sharply, and for a brief moment, she stared at Sarah as if she were a stranger. Then she waved her hand, dismissing Darrien's words. "I know that you are different Sarah. I've always known that, but what are the chances that you are the reincarnated soul of Caroline?"

Sarah opened her mouth to tell her aunt about the vision she'd had in the circle, but changed her mind.

It had been so real!

Yes, it had been real, but was that vision simply a figment of her imagination, brought on by Darrien's suggestion that she was Caroline?

Jeanie patted her hand once more and then got up from her chair and left the room. Soon she returned holding a large wooden box. It was her magic box. The same box that Sarah had been so curious about as a child. Finally, she was going to see what Aunt Jeanie kept in that box.

Jeanie set it on the table and lifted the heavy lid. It was positioned in a way that Sarah could not actually see what was inside, but her aunt was pulling something out. In her hand, she held a dagger made of clear crystal.

"This dagger has been in the family for generations. It is a powerful tool that will help to protect its owner from evil. Now is the time that you should have it." Jeanie explained, placing the dagger in Sarah's hand.

Sarah studied the dagger. Its beauty was stunning. She was in awe at how prisms of color sparkled through the crystal when she held it up to the light. "How do you use it?" Sarah asked.

"Any spell that you work will be twice as powerful, as long as you use this dagger when casting."

"Thank you," Sarah smiled. "It is a gift I will always treasure."

"It can do something else too," Jeanie told her with a wink.

Sarah looked up at her aunt curiously. "What's that?"

"It will call your familiar to you. The helper that will be with you throughout your life."

As soon as Sarah thought about her spirit helper, the name Zaltar popped into her head. "Zaltar," she spoke the name out loud.

A smoky haze began to gather in front of her, slowly taking on the shape of a man. Fascinated, Sarah watched the outline of his body as it turned solid. His hard body was like chiseled stone, his skin stretched tight against his taut muscles. He was pure perfection, with his dark skin and male physique. His black eyes were magical. That was the only word that she could think to describe them.

"You called my lady," he nodded to her.

Sarah was dazed and unable to respond. She knew that witches had familiars, but they were usually cats, or some other type of animal. She'd never heard of a familiar that was a man.

"I'm sorry. I was expecting a cat," she muttered.

I can be whatever my lady would like me to be," he said with a sly smile. He again dematerialized, and became no more than a puff of smoke, before taking the shape of a raven.

"Wow, this is awesome." Sarah laughed. "What is he … a ghost?"

Jeanie cleared her throat. "He is an earth spirit, and will appear in whatever form he can be most helpful. The fact that he appeared in the form of a man, suggests that your hormones are running at full speed." Her aunt gave her a look of disapproval.

"Oh," Sarah blushed.

It was true. She'd practically been on fire since her encounter with Darrien. She guessed that her familiar would accommodate her in those ways too, if she wanted. That he'd appeared in that particular form, made it all too obvious what had been occupying her mind, and now Aunt Jeanie was aware of it.

"Why is it that he has you in such a fever?" Jeanie asked.

Sarah didn't want to answer. How could she tell her aunt that she wanted a vampire, the same vampire whose purpose had been to kill her?

"You don't have to tell me, I think I know," Jeanie said, shaking her head. "He is weaving a spell over you and it's dangerous. A vampire brought your mother a lot of pain, and no doubt it will be the same for you."

Sarah shrugged her shoulders. "It doesn't matter. He said he was going away."

Worry lines creased Jeanie's forehead. "Hmm … well we'll see."

* * * *

The little bell above the door of the Déjà vu tattoo shop jingled as she stepped inside. For the first time since she'd met Dash, he was actually working on a tattoo. A young girl in her early twenties was lying on her stomach in the work chair. It had been placed in a flat position, so that it resembled a small bed.

Dash didn't bother looking up from his task. The small tattoo gun he held in his hand hummed as it moved slowly across skin. Half of the girl's back was covered with tattoos. Nicole could not make out what the tattoos were, but they were full of symbols that appeared to be some type of ancient writing. She was naked from the waist up, wearing only a tight black leather skirt. Her dark hair was styled in two ponytails. The look struck Nicole as too young for the girl's age.

"What do I owe the pleasure," Dash asked her.

The girl looked up and seemed startled to see Nicole standing only a few feet away. "I must be getting rusty, I didn't even smell her," she directed her comment to Dash.

Nicole ignored the girl's obvious reference to her mortal nature. "Dash, I wanted to talk with you about your recipe."

Shocked, he looked up. "You haven't turned have you?"

Nicole shook her head. "I was wondering exactly how you came up with the idea for it?"

Dash shrugged his shoulders. "It just popped into my head on the ride back from Wyoming. Why?"

"I met Ethan's informer. He approached me while I was at the cemetery."

"And?"

"He said that your recipe was a gift from the Place of Light."

Dash jumped up. "I knew it! I knew the recipe was important. Now maybe you'll believe me that we need to do something with it."

"Yuk." The girl in the chair scrunched up her face as if the very thought was nauseating.

"How would you know Sophia? You won't even try it." Dash glared at her.

"Still, it can't be good. It's too cold."

"What is the recipe? What's in it?" Nicole wanted to know.

"Well now that's a secret. If I go giving out the ingredients to my recipe, someone could steal it."

"I'm not going to steal it." Nicole was amused.

"Well then." Dash put a finger to his head, as if he was concentrating intently on trying to remember something. "I believe there's a bit of cow blood, some vitamins, and some liquefied liver. But I can't tell you more than that."

"Okay, but I do think you are meant to do something with that recipe," Nicole told him. Spotting a metal chair placed against the wall, she sat down.

"I could have told you that," Dash said, as if it should have been obvious.

"There's something else. I need to ask you a favor." Nicole approached the subject of the second reason she'd come to Dash's shop.

"Oh no! Whenever you need something, it usually means I'm going to be dodging wooden stakes and holy water." Dash's face twisted in a grimace.

Nicole laughed. "Really Dash, I know you are much braver than you let on."

Dash turned his attention back to the tattoo he was doing. "You think so do you? Well I have news for you. I can't even watch a zombie movie. Those things are creepier than hell."

Again Nicole laughed. "You're kidding right?"

"So what is it you need?"

"I wanted to ask you if you would go to Romania with me … to the Castle Arges. I need to look for Alec. We haven't heard from him since he left."

Sophia started giggled so hard, that Dash had to pull the tattoo gun away from her back.

"You're a mortal and you want to go to the Castle Arges?" The girl's laugher filled the small shop. "Do you have any idea who lives in that castle?"

Nicole shook her head.

"Well I'll tell you," Dash said looking at Nicole as if she'd completely lost her mind. "Luciano lives at the Castle Arges. He makes Omar look like a schoolyard bully. Besides, have you thought that maybe he just doesn't have any cell phone reception where he is? That place is practically at the end of the earth."

"Still, I'm worried," she told him.

"You're just asking for trouble," Dash frowned.

"You don't seriously believe that he's worse than Omar do you?" Nicole was doubtful. She couldn't imagine anyone being worse than her Uncle Omar.

"I don't know about being *worse* than Omar ... if you are asking if he is as evil, but he is deadly. He can kill you without ever touching you."

"Oh come on?" Nicole said in disbelief.

"It's true ... so I think I'll be passing on this trip. I'd prefer to stay home and watch zombie movies all night," Dash smiled. "Besides, I just don't get into that whole Dracula scene."

"Dash, I really don't want to go alone," Nicole urged. "If you come with me I'll help you market your recipe."

This caught Dash's attention. "Really! And you'll talk to your father about it? Maybe get him to try some?"

Nicole nodded.

"Well then ... have you called your travel agent?" he smiled.

"I want to go to!" Sophia jumped up, revealing her small breasts.

Nicole averted her gaze. "As you said, this could be dangerous."

"Oh but I love danger, and I really want to go to Transylvania so I can meet Dracula."

Dash shook his head. "Sophia, Dracula isn't real."

"He is," she scowled.

"No he's not. Some dude just made him up a long time ago," he explained.

"But can I go anyway?" she pouted.

Dash looked to Nicole.

"It's fine with me," she said.

"Okay, but you don't bite anyone on the way. Just stay with me."

"I promise," she smiled.

"We'll leave tomorrow night," Nicole announced. "If that is okay with everyone?"

"Yes, sounds good to me," Dash told her.

"I'll talk to you then." Nicole got to her feet and started to leave.

"Let me walk you out." Dash jumped up from his chair. "I'll be right back," he told Sophia.

He didn't say anything until they had stepped out onto the sidewalk in front of the shop. " I really hate that I can't read you ... because I have to actually ask you. Are you sure you don't mind if she tags along? I know she's a bit naïve. She only turned a few years ago, and I don't think she was all there to begin with."

"Is she your girlfriend Dash?" Nicole teased.

"Well I thought that since you were taken ..."

"She can go," Nicole told him. "I'll see you tomorrow night."

Nicole walked away, disappearing into the darkness.

Chapter Eight

Caroline stared at the blood-covered chicken coop, her fragile features twisting in disgust. All the chickens were dead. The creature had drained their blood. In a feeding frenzy, he'd spilled as much as he'd consumed. Now there would be no eggs to get her through the winter, and no meat to make broth.

"Lord Rousseau!" she called out. "Why do you do this to me? You take my husband, and now you take my livelihood." She did not expect a reply. The predawn sky was already purple with the coming sunrise.

"Come and talk with me Caroline."

The deep voice came from the darkness beyond the barn doors, near the chicken coop.

Caroline shook her head. "You are evil *monsieur.*"

His dark laughter drifted from the barn. "Evil you say? Are you not the witch?"

"I do not kill," she screamed at him.

Again she heard his deep laughter. "A witch and a vampire *mademoiselle* ... two of the most misunderstood creatures on earth. Why can't we be allies?"

"I would not join with evil," she replied, her voice hot with anger.

"Come here Caroline. Let me look at you. Or are you afraid that your powers are not strong enough to hold back a mere vampire?"

Caroline would not let the creature intimidate her. That would be a mistake. She boldly walked to the barn door. He was inside - hidden within the shadows, his only protection from the rising sun.

"Do you think it was my choice to become what I am?" he asked, his voice hard and bitter.

"I do not know," she responded in a steady voice that did not betray her fear.

"I know that you hate me for what I have done, but I must ask for your help Caroline. I must hide from the sun."

Caroline laughed. "Why would I help you? Why wouldn't I just let you perish? It would be a well deserved fate."

"Yes it would be, but I only did it for survival ... and for you." Darrien attempted to defend himself.

The self-loathing in his voice gave Caroline pause.

Darrien continued. "I know you did not love him Caroline. I saw him hitting you ... I heard your baby daughter scream while he was taking you against your will. Is that not also evil?"

Caroline closed her eyes. His words were true. Her love for her husband had faded long ago. Almost from the beginning, he'd proven himself to be a monster. Though Darrien had actually released her from a living hell, she could not let her heart embrace the thought.

"What do you want from me?" she asked.

"Protection from the sun ... that is all. A room that will shield me from the day, until I can find another place to go."

His hand snaked out of the darkness to pull her into the barn. Caroline screamed, but he quickly put a hand over her mouth.

"I will not hurt you," he told her softly - his lips close to her ear.

Caroline's heart was beating so fast that she could hear it pounding in her ears.

Was it fear, or the thrill of being so close to him ... so close to death?

His lips were on her throat, kissing her softly "I could not let him continue to torture you Caroline. When I saw his fists hitting your face, the only thing I could think of was that girl that would pick wildflowers from the fields near our château. The girl that would watch me as I rode by, as if she wanted to say something but never dared."

"You killed him purposely!" Caroline choked on her words.

"Regretfully, I must confess to that slight indiscretion ... that darkness of which I could not contain," he whispered, kissing her neck.

"You followed me here?" she accused, her voice shaking as she tried to ignore her body's response to his touch.

"Yes, I have been watching you for a long time. I watched him court you, marry you, and then take you away. I had to know that you were cared for."

"They all believe you to be dead. I believed you to be dead." The words caught in her throat.

Darrien laughed. "Yes, my father is quite good at cleaning up messes."

"I loved you!" Caroline sobbed, the emotion finally getting the best of her. "And then I thought you were dead. You never came to me."

"Regrettably ... you now know why."

Caroline shook her head. "I was just another commoner ... someone for you to play with."

Darrien lifted her chin so that he could look into her eyes. "You are many things Caroline, but common is not one of them. I would have come for you, but I did not want to bring this darkness into your life."

He pulled her close, wrapping his arms around her. The coolness of his body was repulsive, but yet so erotic. Her body yearned for him, even more than when he'd been a living - breathing man.

The stillness was shattered by the terrified screams of her child. Caroline's heart leaped into her throat. Pulling away from Darrien, she ran for the house.

* * * *

Sarah sat straight up, her screams vibrating off the walls. It took several minutes for her to relax enough to breathe normally. Again she'd dreamt of Caroline, but it had been more like a memory than a dream. She'd been Caroline. She'd felt what Caroline felt, knew what she knew. Sarah was still shaking from the terror she'd felt when she'd heard the child's screams.

Something had happened to that child!

Sarah searched within herself, trying to remember - trying to go back to that lifetime. But everything was a blank after the sound of the child screaming. Taking another deep breath, Sarah tried to calm her frayed nerves.

The room seemed to be closing in on her, making it difficult to breathe. Knowing that she would never get back to sleep, she decided to get some fresh air. Glancing at the clock, she saw that it was only 2:00 AM. Dawn was still a long time away.

Getting on her robe and slippers, Sarah left her room and went out into the garden. Watching the sea had a way of calming the troubled spirit, and she needed that calm right now. Dreaming of Darrien, had only reminded her of his absence and the void that he'd left behind.

She barely knew him, why did it even matter to her?

Because she *did* know him - she loved him once. A little voice whispered in her ear, the truth that her heart had always known, even if she could not remember as Sarah, except for in her dreams.

Less than a quarter mile from the garden was the Sutter Point lighthouse. It had been abandoned for almost a hundred years. But tonight a light was shining at the top of the lighthouse, beaconing to those out at sea, and to her. Sarah stared, wondering if she was seeing things. In all the time she'd lived in Sutter Point, she'd never seen it lit.

A narrow - overgrown path led from the garden to the lighthouse. She and Taylor would play there as children, but they'd never been allowed to go inside. Aunt Jeanie said it was too dangerous. The stairs could be decayed and they might fall through them.

The beam at the top of the lighthouse called to her. She just knew she was supposed to go there. Sarah could think of nothing but finding out who was in there - who was sending out its light to guide her to the antique structure?

Sarah started down the path, heedless of the darkness and the dangers of the night. The sound of the waves gently crashing against the rocks below was calming, lulling her - comforting her fears. From somewhere in the darkness, the hoot of an owl serenaded the night.

The path led away from the house and onto the point. The lighthouse stood on a large cliff outcropping, where it overlooked the Pacific Ocean. Weeds caught in her slippers, making the trek more difficult, but Sarah barely noticed this. She kept walking, as if driven by some magnetic force that she was completely unaware of.

Reaching the lighthouse, she peered up, expecting to see light flashing from the windows at the top of the structure, but it was dark.

Had she imagined the light? Was she really asleep, and this was just another bizarre dream?

Sarah made her way to the large door that was always kept locked. It stood open just a crack, the rusty chain and padlock lay on the ground in front of it.

Someone was in there, or had been.

Reaching out, Sarah slowly pushed the door open. The old hinges creaked so loudly that it undoubtedly alerted whoever was inside, of her presence. Even this knowledge did not deter her. Stepping inside, she found herself in almost complete darkness. A small amount of moonlight came in from the top of the lighthouse, illuminating the long - spiral staircase.

Placing her foot on the first step, Sarah cringed when the wood moaned loudly beneath her weight. Holding onto the rail, she took the steps slowly, waiting for one to give way and send her falling to her death.

Finally she reached the lantern room. An abundance of moonlight found its way in through the storm panes, making it easier to see. Clearly no one was there but herself. At least that is what she initially believed. As she peered around the room, her eyes caught the movement of a shadow. Then she realized that it wasn't a shadow at all, but a figure standing at the window, looking out at the sea.

Darrien had called for her!

Her heart jumped at the thought, while at the same time her senses were screaming at her - telling her to run and hide. The figure turned to look at her. His eyes were alight, not with hunger. but with the thirst for fear. It would feed off of her terror, as well as the warm blood that flowed through her veins. The evil in those eyes was foreign to her - they were not Darrien's eyes. This creature was a vampire, but he wasn't Darrien.

Sarah's screams sounded hollow in the glass enclosure. She tried to turn and run, but was shaking so badly that her legs did not want to move. She felt in the pocket of her robe for her dagger, but it wasn't there. Since receiving the dagger, she'd made a habit of taking it with her wherever she went, but this time she'd forgotten.

She searched her memory for some type of spell that would ward the creature off, but she drew a blank. She just hadn't paid enough attention to her aunt's spells.

He stepped closer, but his movements were slow. He was in no hurry. The longer she had to feel fear before her death, the more enjoyable the experience would be for him.

Sarah willed her legs to move and she ran toward the staircase, taking the stairs two at a time. She was breathless when she reached the bottom. Stealing a look over her shoulder, she sighed in relief to see that he wasn't there. Her reprieve was short-lived. When she turned to look in front of her, the creature was there - blocking her way to the door. His movements had been so fast that her brain hadn't even registered the fact that he'd flown down the stairs ahead of her.

A scream of utter terror ripped from her throat. This did not faze the vampire. He smiled ghoulishly, enjoying her fear - feeding off of it.

Out of pure desperation, Sarah held out her hand and pulled at the energy around her. She gathered the earth's energy into her fingers and directed it at her attacker. Suddenly the vampire was knocked off balance. It wasn't much, but enough to give her time to slip by him and out the door.

As she ran, her slippers caught on the weeds, tripping her. Sarah fell hard to the ground, catching herself with her hands. The skin on her hands was scraped and bleeding, but there was no time to think about that, or to feel the pain. She jumped up and kicked the slippers from her feet.

Her efforts were in vain. The creature now blocked the path ahead of her. In the moonlight she could make out a deformed forehead and the way his cheekbones protruded so far that it appeared as if they would tear the flesh on his face. His lips were drawn back, revealing deadly fangs. The glowing redness in his eyes reminded her of a demon - a true spawn of the prince of darkness.

He moved toward her and her screams rang through the air, shattering the peaceful silence of the night. Looking around frantically, Sarah searched for some place to run - some way that she could escape, but she was trapped. The only place to run was over the cliffs and into the sea.

There was a flash of movement - so subtle that she might have thought it a trick of the eyes, if not for the fact that now the vampire lay on the ground, struggling with an assailant.

Her relief was so complete that she felt her knees grow weak. At that moment, she wanted nothing more than to sink to the ground and let the fear fade from her heart.

Darrien tore at the vampire's throat, but as quickly as the blood spurted from the wound, it began to heal. He would have to sever the head to kill the other vampire. Sarah searched the ground for some type of weapon, a stick or branch that she could use to pierce the vampire's heart.

From the dark sky, a large raven swooped toward her, dropping the crystal dagger at her feet. Sarah picked it up and ran toward the vampire. As soon as she had a clear shot at the vampire's chest, she buried the sharp end of the dagger into his heart. Instantly the dagger began to glow with a black light that slowly turned red and then blue. The light was so bright that it cut through the darkness around them.

Startled, Darrien backed away. The light from the dagger became so brilliant that Sarah had to shield her eyes from the glare. Then it was gone. All that was left of the vampire was a pile of ash.

Darrien looked over at her. "What was that?"

Sarah stepped to the white pile of ash that had once been a vampire, and retrieved her dagger. She held it up so that Darrien could see it. "It was a gift from my aunt."

Darrien stared at the magical weapon that Sarah held in her hand.

"My familiar, Zaltar must have known that I would need it, so he brought it to me," she told him.

"Well I have to say it works much better than a wooden stake, which doesn't work at all by the way. Just so you know, in case this ever happens again." Darrien encircled her waist with his arms.

Sarah gazed into his eyes. "I thought you were going away?"

A smile touched his lips. "Did you really think that I would leave you to these ghouls?"

Before she could answer, he leaned down and brushed her lips with a soft kiss. "We should get you home now. I need to talk with your aunt and see if she will convince you to go away from here."

Sarah shook her head. "You will only worry her."

"Someone has to talk some sense into you." Again he kissed her, but this time with more heat. His tongue licked at her lips, parting them so that he could explore her mouth - tasting her. His need surrounded her - burrowing into her pores until she felt the fire spread through her body and into her groin. The wet fire between her legs was agony.

His arms tightened around her and he devoured her lips with his. Then she felt the ground give way beneath her feet. They were ascending into the dark sky - into the billowing black clouds that were starting to gather over the sea. Sarah held onto him tightly, not caring that she was hundreds of feet in the air, or that she was in the arms of an immortal.

When she looked at him, she did not see a creature of the night, but a being of pure beauty and divine wisdom. She saw her knight.

Slowly he brought her to the ground. Sarah recognized the shrub maze in her aunt's garden. They were in the grass, the tall shrubs shielding them from sight. He leaned over her - a silhouette against the moon. Though a cloud partially obscured the moon's light, it was still bright enough to see everything around her. The silver beams were magical somehow, as if it was all meant to be, the enchantment - the danger, and her passion for this immortal.

She was on fire. Sarah felt as if she would disintegrate if he did not quench her thirst. Again he kissed her, his mouth sucking at her tongue - devouring her mouth as he devoured her soul. His lips were on her throat - his tongue licking at her flesh.

She felt his hand slide up her leg, lifting the hem of her nightgown to expose her thighs. He removed her panties so gracefully that she barely felt them come off, but she could sense his gaze on the glistening wetness between her legs.

His mouth was on her thighs, licking and teasing her until she began to tremble with the power of her need. Then she felt the sensation of sharp pain when his fangs slit through her skin. As warm blood dripped from her wounds, he gently licked it away. The act was so erotic that it nearly brought her to a shattering orgasm.

"I can't take this,' she breathed.

His dark laughter floated on the night air, enchanting her further.

She felt his cool fingers rubbing the swollen lips between her legs, and she arched her hips to him. Darrien obliged, slipping his fingers into her molten core.

Sarah moaned loudly. The sensation of his fingers moving within her, as he licked and bit at her flesh, was total ecstasy.

"I want you," she gasped, moving her hips in rhythm to his probing fingers.

The moistness between her legs turned to liquid fire as he brought her the release that she so desperately needed. The pleasure was so unbelievable that she could not stop the screams that escaped her lips.

She felt him move away from her, but for the moment all she could do was close her eyes and try to bring her breathing under control. All around her the night seemed to be alive with sound. In the distance, she could hear the roar of the sea and a gust of wind disturbed the shrubs that surrounded them. The sound of the blood rushing through his body was bewitching – it called to her - tempting her.

Sarah sat up and grabbed his arm. She could think of nothing but tasting his blood on her tongue. Baring her teeth, she prepared to sink them into his flesh, but he pulled away from her abruptly.

Darrien stared at her in shock. The horror on his face would have been comical, if not for her insatiable hunger for his blood.

"Sarah stop!" he hissed.

Sarah blinked as if coming awake. She reached out for him, but he backed away from her.

Pain wrapped around her heart and squeezed until she felt as if she would die. "What have I done?"

The expression on his face softened and he pulled her into his arms. "It is not what you have done, but what I have done."

Sarah shook her head, confused by his words.

"You are turning Sarah." His words were full of all of the horror she'd seen on his face when he'd looked at her.

"I'm becoming a vampire?" she asked.

"Yes," he answered, the agony he was feeling caused his voice to crack as he spoke.

"Because you fed from me?" she asked, her fear at battle with her desire to understand.

He nodded. "But there is something wrong. It shouldn't have happened unless you fed on my blood."

Sarah was speechless. Had she given up her life to be loved by him? Did she even care?

"It seems to be happening slowly. Probably since the first time I pierced your skin." Darrien seemed to be talking more to himself than to her, as he tried to make sense out of what was happening.

A million thoughts raced through her mind. Foremost among them, was the sun. Would she ever see the sun again?

"I have to take you some place safe, and I have to go away from you," he declared. "Maybe it isn't permanent yet. You recovered from your hunger last time."

Sarah shook her head. "I would prefer to turn than be away from you."

"No you wouldn't."

"Why didn't you make love to me?" she asked, realizing for the first time that he had not really taken her completely.

A deep sadness entered his eyes. "I could not do it to you again Caroline ... I mean Sarah," he corrected himself quickly.

Sarah was shocked by his words, though she knew she should not have been. Even as he had brought her such pleasure, in his mind - she was Caroline. She got to her feet and turned away from him. She shook with the effort it took to keep her anger and hurt from erupting.

"I'm sorry Sarah. I know you don't believe that you are Caroline, but I know that you are. I can feel it whenever I am with you." He tried to reason with her.

"You are delusional," she told him, her voice hard and unyielding. "Go away Darrien. Go dream about Caroline and leave me be." Sarah walked away, without looking back at him.

"Sarah please … you are still in danger," he called after her.

Sarah did not turn around - she did not even let herself listen to his words.

"Don't go into the light Sarah," he yelled. "It will make you sick and could kill you."

Sarah left him in the shrub maze and ran to the comfort of home. With each step she took, another piece of her heart seemed to fall away from her.

Chapter Nine

Glancing at her watch, Nicole saw that it was nearly 9:00 PM. Already late, she took the stairs two at a time. The French Quarter building where Ethan kept his office was beautiful, though she wished that she lived a little closer. Having a boss that was a vampire had some advantages, but having her nights free was not of them. She often worked long hours at night, helping Ethan with whatever project he was working on. Right now that happened to be the disappearance of a little boy.

Ethan's contacts in the police department thought the boy's disappearance might be connected to vampires, but Nicole didn't think so. This crime had predator written all over it - the human predator variety. That wasn't to say that there were not plenty of deaths that could be attributed to vampires.

Most of the members of the New Orleans Police Department were unaware of the vampires that roamed their city, but there were a couple of officers that knew, and they would seek out Ethan's help. Those in the police department that knew the truth about the death that plagued their city, welcomed Ethan's expertise.

Ethan was a Light Seeker, a vampire that fed on animals while searching for a way to end their curse. Ending the curse of the vampire, and finding the Place of Light was one of Ethan's ongoing projects, and the one that Nicole spent most of her time on.

She knew Ethan was busy right now with the boy's disappearance, and she hoped that he wouldn't have a problem with her leaving for Romania.

Reaching the top of the stairs, Nicole frowned. The office door was shut. Ethan always kept it open when he was in. From behind the door she could hear the soft murmur of voices. She brought her hand up to knock, but hesitated. If the door was closed, Ethan obviously didn't want to be disturbed.

Finally she knocked, knowing that she didn't have a choice. She had to tell Ethan she was leaving.

A moment later the door opened and Ethan stood there, staring at her. "Why didn't you just come in?"

"I thought you might be busy."

Ethan motioned for her to enter and then shut the door. Nicole was startled to see the lycan sitting in front of Ethan's desk.

"Well hello again," he smiled.

"Hi,' she greeted him, unsure of what else to say.

"Lex has some news for us," Ethan informed her.

"I have information that the Fabre Witches relocated to the coast of Oregon, in a small town called Sutter Point," Lex explained.

"That's fantastic," Nicole smiled. Finally they had found one of her sisters.

"I thought we would leave right away," Ethan started pacing the floor. "If we know where she is, Omar probably does too. We'll have to get to her soon … if it's not already too late."

"What about the case you are working on?" she asked.

"They found the boy. He was still alive, but barely. They've already booked someone for the crime, and it wasn't a vampire."

"I suspected as much," Nicole told him. "But thank God they found him alive."

"Now we can focus on this business of going to Oregon," Ethan was digging through some paperwork on his desk.

Nicole didn't respond. She knew that her first obligation was to ensure her sister's safety, but her fear for Alec made her pause.

"Is something wrong?" Ethan asked.

"I haven't heard from Alec since he left. I thought I should go to Romania," Nicole told him, her eyes downcast.

Ethan shook his head. "I knew it was foolish for him to go there alone."

"I may have a solution." Lex said as he stood up. "I will go to Sutter Point and see to the girl's safety. It would do no good to bring her back here to New Orleans. She'd just be closer to Omar here. Let me convince her to go someplace where she can safely wait until the time that all three of you can be brought together."

"Where will she go?" Nicole was hesitant. Lex seemed like an ally, but she could not forget that he was a lycan, and an enemy of her kind.

"Don't worry, I have a place in mind. In the meantime, you can go fetch your friend. Soon you will need all the friends you can get." Lex's voice held a cryptic note.

"You'll contact Ethan as soon as you've found her?" Nicole asked him, still unsure if she should leave the fate of her sister to a stranger.

Lex seemed to guess what she was thinking. "Don't worry. Her safety is as important to me, as it is you."

Nicole smiled. "Thank you."

Ethan looked at Nicole. "You are not thinking of going to Romania alone, are you?"

She shook her head. "Dash and his girlfriend are coming with me."

"Hmm ... well that's comforting," Ethan frowned.

"I know you think he's odd, but Dash is a great friend. He's someone I would like on my side," Nicole said, draping an arm over Ethan's shoulder. "Besides, I told him we could help him market his recipe if he came with me."

"We!" Ethan's mouth dropped open. "You won't get anyone to try that stuff."

"Actually," Lex interrupted. "As I told your young lady friend ... that recipe is important to the future of your kind."

"You see," Nicole grinned. "I do actually know what I'm doing."

* * * *

A shroud of darkness wrapped around her - squeezing at her chest until she felt as if she would smother. Though she could not actually see the dark entity, for Sarah it was real. The darkness was the heartache and despair of yearning for an immortal - someone that could never come into the light. There was despair in knowing that she may herself, be forever destined to darkness.

With her legs drawn up to her chest, Sarah huddled in the corner of the dank cellar. No light could reach her in the earthen basement. She'd reached the house just before dawn, and had gone straight for the basement. It was the only safe place to hide from the light.

She could hear Jeanie in the kitchen, the floor creaking as she moved about, probably preparing breakfast. Her aunt would not realize that she was gone until she went upstairs to see what was keeping Sarah from breakfast. Jeanie would be frantic.

The last thing that she wanted to do was worry her aunt anymore than she already had.

"Aunt Jeanie," Sarah called out weakly.

There was no chance that her aunt had heard from the kitchen. The house was too solid - the floors too thick.

"Aunt Jeanie!" Sarah called again, this time with a much louder voice.

The sound of Jeanie's footsteps stopped.

"I'm down here!" Sarah screamed with as much strength as she could muster.

Though it was only a short time, it seemed like an eternity before the basement door opened and a sliver of light penetrated the darkness. Sarah scrambled away from the light, terrified that it would burn her if she came into contact with it.

"Sarah, are you down here?" Jeanie asked, the uncertainty in her voice making it sound feeble.

"I'm here. Shut the door quickly!"

Jeanie switched on the light that hung from a fixture above the stairs. Stepping onto the top stair, she pulled the door shut behind her.

"Sarah, what are you doing down here in the dark?"

"I have to talk to you," Sarah told her aunt, her voice shaking.

Jeanie started down the stairs, her hand grasping the rail. When she was halfway down the staircase, she saw her niece huddled in the corner. Sarah knew she was a sight with her feet bare, and her nightgown torn and dirty.

"Oh my! What's happened to you?" Jeanie hurried down the stairs to Sarah.

"I've turned," Sarah told her softly.

"What do you mean you've turned?" Jeanie's brows came together in confusion.

"I'm just turning ... becoming a vampire." Sarah told her, squeezing her eyes closed so that she would not have to see the disappointment on her aunt's face.

"He bit you again, didn't he? Where did he bite you?" Jeanie was examining Sarah's throat.

"Not there," Sarah said, shaking her head.

"Where then?" Jeanie wanted to know.

Sarah didn't answer. She didn't want to tell her aunt about what had happened between her and Darrien. Jeanie picked up on Sarah's reluctance, and guessed why she was unwilling to show her where she'd been bitten.

Clucking her tongue, Jeanie shook her head in annoyance. "You didn't listen to a word I said about being careful."

"I'm sorry," Sarah sobbed. "When I'm with him ... it's like nothing else matters."

"It's the vampire's spell," Jeanie told her sternly. "This is why I told you that it was dangerous for you to be with him too much."

"But I didn't feed on him! This shouldn't have happened," Sarah insisted.

"Maybe it hasn't happened. Maybe it's all in your head," Jeanie suggested, a look of hope in her eyes.

"I've hungered for his blood. It's like ... it takes control of me and I don't know what I am doing. But he stopped me before I could feed from him."

"That could be an instinct born into you."

"He told me that it's happening slowly. He told me to stay out of the light."

"Well at least he thought that much about it," Jeanie said, sarcasm dripping from her words.

"What am I going to do?"

"There isn't much you *can* do ... if indeed you have been turned, but I have my doubts."

The uncertainty in Jeanie's eyes was like a ray of hope to Sarah. She did not like the idea of being condemned to a dark cellar for the rest of her life. "How can we know?"

"Come upstairs into the light. That is the best test I can think of."

Sarah shook her head violently. "No! He told me that the sunlight could kill a vampire."

"It is true that too much sunlight can kill a vampire, but if there is only a little exposure, it could make you ill, but probably wouldn't kill you."

"No. We need to find some other way." Sarah was adamant.

"Very well." Jeanie stood up. "I'll bring you some food and water, and you can stay down here until I can figure something out."

* * * *

It was nearly midday, but the murky clouds coming in from the sea were like a blanket of night covering the sun. It might as well have been twilight. The old Victorian mansion almost appeared to watch him, as if it had a life of its own. With his enhanced senses, he could hear it breathing - daring him to come forth and save the witch. At least this is what he sensed, but he realized it wasn't the house at all. It was his self-doubt.

Was he worthy?

Did he really have it in him to be selfless enough to save the witch and find redemption for his efforts?

Lex closed his eyes, trying to block out those images that haunted his every waking moment.

He knew firsthand how darkness could cloud one's judgment and eventually take over. This was what was happening with Omar. Lex didn't know what drove the darkness within the ancient vampire, but the result would be the same. Evil would eventually consume Omar, like it had almost consumed him - eating away at his soul until he had nearly killed his own daughter.

Lex had not spoken with Kayla since he'd been banished from *Outerlands*, nor had he gone near his adopted granddaughter - the girl that was the third sister. The one he most needed to protect. Although this self-imposed isolation from his family was punishment enough to bring him to his knees, it came nowhere near to the anguish or self-loathing he felt for the things that he could never take back.

His darkest hour was as clear today as it had been that night years ago. The scene replayed in his mind a hundred times a day. Even now the memory intruded and he lost focus of his purpose for being in Sutter Point. The house faded from his sight, replaced by those haunting memories.

The flames that leaped out from the pit, cast the large earthen chamber in deep orange and red light. It was hot - so hot that it could have been the entrance to the underworld.

Lex's dark hair hung in sweat soaked strands around his head. Shedding his robe, he stood naked, except for a black cotton breechcloth.

In his hands he held a golden cube. The cube bore markings similar to Egyptian hieroglyphics. With the square shaped box tightly clenched in both hands, he raised it high above his head and closed his eyes. "With this key ... Lord of Darkness ... I call on you to close the door to *Ourterlands* from all other worlds."

The earth rumbled within the rock chamber, sending stones flying toward him. Then there was only silence.

At that point, he still had not been strong enough to draw the dark energy into the Rostin, that magic key to all dimensions. Even after years of preparing, somehow his energy was still being drawn away from him.

Lex was back in the present. He squeezed his eyes shut and tried to block out the picture of evil that he had once been. It didn't work. Once again he was cast back in time to that night.

He remembered thinking that the reason that he had been unsuccessful in his endeavor to close the door to *Outerlands* was because Vance had betrayed him. Vance had been one of his fiercest warriors, and he also happened to be the man that his daughter loved.

Lex had come to believe that his memory of Brenda was causing his failure. Kayla's mother had been the only light that still burned in his heart, and he had worried that he might need to kill her before enough of the dark energy filled his soul to give him the strength he needed?

He had been so close - too close.

He had though that if he could kill Vance and Kayla, he would finally be at peace with the world of humans. Maybe then he could put his energy into closing the doors and isolating mankind.

It was for the good of the people.

The humans were too primitive to coexist with those of *Outerlands*. Since he could not seem to stop the crossing over into that world, he would close the door and rule *Outerlands* without the taint of humans.

Lex forced the memory from his mind. He hadn't known then that Brenda's child was his own daughter, and that by harming Vance he would be bringing heartache to his child. He'd believed Brenda had betrayed him with a human.

It was true that she'd been terrified of what he was. She could not accept that he was of the wolves, and this was why she'd kept the knowledge of their child to herself. If he could only go back to that moment, he would change so many things. He would not have brought such horrific pain to his daughter, or to his people - the people he had been sworn to protect as the leader of the Zen Warrior Society.

To this day, he still could not believe that before he'd known that Kayla was his daughter, he'd actually planned on having her assassinated. Lex shuddered to think of how close he'd come to killing his only child. If it had not been for the Valley of Dreams, he may have done just that.

The Valley of Dreams was a fog-covered basin where one would lose themselves within their own fantasies and fears. It was one of the most avoided places in *Outerlands*. One could enter the Valley of Dreams and wander around within their head until they perished from exposure or starvation.

He had planned on killing her, but she'd saved him from himself, and the mist. Lex could not block out that memory, no matter how he tried.

Kayla had been running from him. She ran through the forest. Far away - the ethereal mist of the Valley of Dreams beckoned her, and she ran faster. The Zen warriors were bigger and stronger, accustomed to the wolf's body. They were gaining on her fast - closing the gap.

The mist was not so far away when one could maneuver the woods with the keen senses of the beast. The fingers of the enchanting white fog reached out into the woods to touch her with its magic, tapping into her brain to show her what could be hers.

"Do not go in there Kayla," Lex's words followed her as she let the mist close in around her.

His transformation back to human form was complete, and he watched - horrified as his newfound daughter entered the mist. His warriors had stopped some distance behind him, refusing to go further.

Lex moved cautiously into the mist. "Kayla!" he called out. "You cannot stay in the mist. You will die in here!"

A shadow moved within the mist and Lex walked toward it. As the milky air cleared, he saw Brenda. She looked exactly the same as she did the last day he'd set eyes on her. She was crying, and shaking her head in disappointment.

"Brenda!" Her name slipped from his lips. "You are not real," he yelled, closing his eyes against the vision.

When he opened his eyes Brenda was gone, but now there was a little girl riding a squeaky tricycle. She was circling him. The child stopped and with a small - plump hand, brushed her blond curls away from her face. She looked up at him with wide blue eyes.

"Daddy ... where were you? Why do you want to hurt me?"

Lex swallowed hard, the pain of realization tearing at his heart. The mists swirled around him, seeping into his mouth, his nose, and ears. It was even oozing through his skin. Every moment he'd every spent with Brenda moved through his brain, and then there was the child, his only child.

"I'm so sorry. I just didn't know!" he pleaded with the little girl for understanding.

A large wolf came out of the mist - baring its teeth, it snarled sadistically. The beast jumped on the child, sinking its teeth into her throat. The wolf began to twist its head back and forth - tearing at her flesh.

"Stop!" Lex screamed and ran toward the animal.

In that instant, the hatred and darkness fled his heart, replaced with an all-consuming instinct to protect his child.

The vision dissipated, leaving in its place nothing but empty space. Lex collapsed to the ground. "Kayla!" he called out.

"Lex." The sound of someone calling his name came from everywhere at the same time.

The Gatekeeper stepped out of the thick mist, his broad mouth spreading into a bright smile.

"You are not real," Lex choked out the words.

"I am as real as you. This is something you have forgotten."

"What do you want?"

"To talk," Sirus told him.

"Go away! Leave me to my hellish torment, as it is well deserved."

"Yes, it is." The Gatekeeper agreed with him. "But I want to talk of second chances."

Lex shook his head and turned away.

"You will put yourself at the mercy of the people you had hoped to betray."

The Gatekeeper disappeared as quickly as the last vision. Lex shook inside, no longer sure of what was real and what was illusion.

Slender hands grabbed his arm and began pulling him. Lex followed, no longer caring where it was he was going. Slowly the mist thinned until he found himself in the crisp night air.

Kayla stared up at him, her bright blue eyes wary - ready for him to leap at her. What clothes remained on her - hung in shreds. The consequence of the changing when one was not ready for it.

"You came back for me!"

Kayla nodded her head, but still she watched him cautiously.

That had been the moment that he'd truly embraced her as his daughter, but it had been too late. He'd already stolen from her the only thing that would matter in her life - the man that she loved.

Chapter Ten

Jeanie cleared her throat in an attempt to get the man's attention. She'd put on her hooded cloak and left the house so that she could seek out help for Sarah, but she'd noticed him across the road - staring. When Jeanie approached the man, he seemed to be completely unaware of her presence.

Now the man was looking at her. His eyes were full of confusion, as if he'd just been awakened from a deep sleep.

"Can I help you with something?" she asked.

Now his eyes were sharp and alert. "I'm looking for the Fabre family."

"For what reason?" Jeanie's eyes narrowed on him.

"It is a sensitive matter that I must discuss with the family. Do you know them?"

"Maybe," Jeanie was cautious.

"A young girl of the family is in extreme danger. I must speak with her." It was obvious that he was getting impatient.

"Well you're a day late and a dollar short." Jeanie was in a huff, irritated by the constant intrusion of these otherworldly creatures in the affairs of the Fabre family. She knew that he could not be human. If he were, he would not know about Sarah being in danger.

* * * *

Caroline's heart raced, threatening to burst in her chest. She slammed against the cottage door - practically ripping it from its hinges to get inside. It was still dark within the confines of the cottage walls. She had not yet drawn back the curtains to let in the morning sun. Her eyes scanned the interior until they came to rest on the cradle where her baby daughter lay screaming in terror.

At first she could see nothing but the small form of the baby lying on her back, her arms swinging in the air as she screamed. When her eyes adjusted to the dim lighting, she saw that there was an area of darkness that was denser that the natural darkness. The shadow stood near the cradle - staring down at the frantic child.

"What are you? What do you want?" Caroline demanded.

The thick darkness that was the shadow - moved. It was then that Caroline saw red glowing eyes where its head should have been. Yelping, she backed away from the evil presence.

"I have come to offer you a reprieve." The rasping - hollow voice was the voice of evil in its purest form. It was a voice that could not be heard with the ears, but only within the mind. "I will spare you your fate, in exchange for the child."

Caroline prayed for the strength to face down this being - this bringer of death. "Why would you have an interest in this baby?" she asked, refusing to show fear.

The silence that followed was like that of the grave. The shadow hovered over the cradle, but its orbs of red light were fixed on Caroline.

Caroline shook her head. "If you have come for me … then take me, but leave my child be."

Its hollow laughter filled her head. "When you embrace death you seek me out. You have made your choice. If you seek immortality, you will be trading the child's life for your own."

Caroline blinked and the shadow was gone. As quickly as the presence left, the child became quiet, falling into a deep slumber. She ran to the baby and reached out to feel the child's chest. Sighing with relief that the baby was still breathing.

Swallowing hard, Caroline was confused by the words of the entity. Had she just come face to face with the Angel of Death? Or was it some demon sent to bring death and misfortune to her family? Whatever it was, it wanted her child?

* * * *

Sarah jumped upon waking. Her dream of Caroline remained vivid in her mind. It was the curse of the Fabre witches to remain alone throughout life. If they tried to defy the curse, they risked the lives of their children. Most women in her family never married. If they did, the marriage rarely lasted. They feared for their children, and like most mothers, they would ultimately choose their children over their own hearts.

No one knew the origins of the curse, but at least now Sarah knew that it must have come before Caroline's time. It was the curse that had brought about her demise, not Darrien.

Sarah's thoughts were brought back to the present when she heard a noise at the top of the stairs. She held her breath and listened.

The door handle rattled and then turned.

Scrambling to the other side of the basement, Sarah tried to avoid the dim light that made its way into the basement from the open door. Her senses picked up danger, even before she saw the figure on the stairs. It was a man, but at the same time, he wasn't a man. The instinct that she was born with screamed at her to run. That instinct told her that this was a monster, someone that she should fear. But Jeanie stood behind him, and she didn't seem the least bit worried.

Her eyes followed him as he made his way down the stairs. Silently she waited - waited for him to reveal who he was - waited for the death that she sensed was imminent.

The man stood there staring at her. Not with hatred and hunger as she'd expected. What she saw in his eyes was understanding and compassion.

"My name is Lex."

Sarah didn't respond. She continued to watch him, wary of any sudden movements.

"I am not here to hurt you. I have come to help you."

"And how do you think you can do that?" Sarah finally broke her silence.

"I know that you can sense that I am different, but you don't know why. Am I correct so far?" he asked.

Sarah nodded.

Jeanie stood behind the man, saying nothing.

"I am of the wolf people," he told her. "Have you ever heard of lycans?"

Sarah again nodded. This was another mythical creature that she had not considered real. Just like she had believed that vampires were no more than myth.

"That is what I am. I don't have time to explain everything right now, but that is what I am." Lex held out a hand to her.

Reluctantly, Sarah placed her hand in his and let him pull her to her feet. When her skin made contact with his, she saw into his head and into his heart. The room seemed to fade away and she stepped into someone else's body - into someone else's head. The vision was so strong that it blinded her to the world around her.

* * * *

Sarah was in the body of the man's daughter, and she was on the ground, sobbing.

"I am so sorry for your loss." A man with dark hair tried to soothe her. She didn't know who it was, but he seemed to be someone important.

Then she could hear someone else's voice. "We tried, but he lost too much blood by the time we got here." Whoever was talking to her was male, and she felt as if she should know him.

Her tears fell, heedless of all else. What did she care of what others thought? Her heart was gone, stolen from her once again.

The man was there, the same man that had entered her aunt's basement. He stepped forward, putting a hand gently on her shoulder. "I am so sorry. I cannot change what has already happened, but I can make amends by being the father I should have been long ago."

Sarah stepped back into her own body and was looking upon a scene that she was not part of. A young woman was crying hysterically.

The woman shook her head violently. "You have caused me too much grief. It is you that took from me those that I loved," she told him, crying out in anguish. "My dad is a man of God, you are a creature of darkness."

Lex bowed his head and backed away from her. "If you should need me Kayla, I will do my best," he told her before leaving through the open door of the death chamber where her lover's body lay on a cold slab of marble - covered with a red velvet cloth.

Pulling away from a large man with blond hair, the woman made her way to where the body of her lover lay. She then dropped to her knees beside him.

Sarah could feel her grief, and it was so great that it shook her to the core. The woman could only lay her head on the body of her lover and cry. She was not aware of when the others left the room so that she could be alone with her love for the last time.

Sarah was still Sarah, but she was also the young woman at the same time. She could feel what the woman felt - knew what she knew.

The minutes ticked by but she was unaware of it. She lost herself in the memory of her lover. She remembered the last words he'd spoken to her.

I do love you angel.

While Sarah was in the other girl's body, she felt as if she was just as responsible for his death as Lex was.

Lex's voice tore her from her thoughts of embracing death. "Kayla … let me help."

"You have done enough dear father!"

"Even during his darkest hour … he would not denounce his love for you,' Lex told her, his voice soft with regret.

The girl then turned to face him, furious blue sparks flying from her eyes. "So you killed him!"

"The one who did this … was someone else. He was corrupt with hate and envy of another man," Lex stepped closer to her. "I see that monster entering your soul daughter. Do not let hate twist its way into your heart."

Kayla was silent, staring straight ahead. She could no longer see Lex, but only the bleakness of a future without love.

"Daughter … I think there is a way I can help."

Her eyes strayed to his face, but they were unyielding.

* * * *

Unexpectedly, Sarah found herself back in the moment and the scene in her head was gone. The man had released her hand, but not before she had seen his dark secrets. Now she knew why he was here. He wanted redemption.

She felt something else. She had been shown the girl's sorrow and loss for a reason. It was a warning - an omen.

"You killed your daughter's lover," she accused. "And now you seek forgiveness by saving me."

A mixture of shock and sorrow clouded the man's features. "You are a very talented young woman, but you do not know the whole story" he told her. "It makes no difference. With the power of both the immortal and the witch, I can see how you would be such an asset."

"To this battle between the sisters and the vampires?" Sarah asked, turning away from him. She did not believe that she was strong enough to do battle with the evil that pursued her.

"I can see someone has been talking to you," he told her.

"If you had hoped to save me, you are too late," she stated.

"You have taken a vampire for a lover, and you believe he's turned you?"

Sarah looked to Jeanie, realizing that her aunt had already confessed her secrets to this stranger.

"What is it that you want?" Sarah asked him.

"To keep you safe until you can unite with your sisters."

Sarah laughed. "As I said, you are too late. I have already been brought into darkness."

"And you are sure of this?" he said, arching one brow.

"Yes! I hunger for blood."

"That could be because you are a born vampire. This doesn't necessarily make you a full fledged bloodsucker."

"And how would you know?" Sarah asked sarcastically. She wasn't sure if she was angry for the intrusion, or she was beginning to accept her fate and did not appreciate the lycan's efforts to save her from the inevitable. At least if she had turned, she could go to Darrien and he would have no reason to turn her away. Of course this would do nothing to cure him of his delusion that she was Caroline.

Lex held out his hand. "Come with me into the light. If my suspicions are correct, you will be fine."

Sarah shook her head. Why should she trust this stranger, this lycan? He was a natural born enemy of the vampire.

"I believe that you were born with a natural resistance to the poison of the vampire," Lex voiced his thoughts. "If this is true, it makes you an even more valuable asset to the cause."

"What does it matter? They will only find another way to be rid of me?" Sarah looked away.

"I can take you somewhere where you will have some protection from Omar's followers," he told her. "I can take you to your sisters when the time is right, but first you must take my hand."

She still hesitated. Finally Sarah allowed him to lead her into the light that was coming through the open basement door. She braced herself for the blistering heat and the scorching of her skin, but nothing happened.

"Now let's go upstairs," he urged.

Sarah followed him up the stairs and into the kitchen. Again she felt nothing. She was no different than she had been the day before.

"Why would I crave blood?" she asked.

"I will explain everything, but you may want to cleanup and dress first," he advised.

* * * *

From St. Peter's Square the view of the Vatican was ethereal, almost eerie in a way. He stood next to a large fountain. Water gushed from the top of the fountain and spilled over the sides of the marble. Illuminated by pale yellow light, the water resembled liquid gold.

At this late hour, few visitors remained in St. Peter's Square. Alec's eyes scanned the faces of the people that were still milling about, wondering which of them might be his contact.

Father Rovati had reluctantly promised to meet Alec in the square, but that was only because the good father had no idea that he was meeting with a vampire - one of the foulest creatures to ever roam the earth, at least according to the church.

The priest approached him from behind, but Alec was not taken by surprise. His keen sense of hearing had detected the man's footsteps from quite a distance away.

"Mr. Norwood?" the man asked, his voice firm and confident.

He turned around to face the priest. Alec was a sight with his long hair blowing in the soft night breeze, and the way the light reflected in his icy blue eyes – eyes that were distinctively those of a vampire. The average person would have thought Alec was different, maybe even attractively so, but the good father was not the average person. No, this priest was the advisor to His Holiness the Pope, in all things paranormal.

The priest stood at least a good foot shorter than Alec. The black coat the man was wearing seemed almost too warm for the season. His short-cropped silver hair and the deep crows feet around his eyes told Alec that Father Rovati was well beyond his prime, but the man's dark eyes were sharp, and he knew what Alec was.

"How dare you come to this holy place?" Fury oozed from the man's words.

"I come seeking your help," Alec told him with a smile.

"What help could I possibly be to a creature of evil?" Father Rovati's eyes followed Alec's every move, but he did not back away, nor did he show any sign that he was ready to flee.

"Is it not your job ... your mission in life to be a savior of souls?" Alec asked him.

"I fear your soul was lost long ago," the priest told him.

"Among those in Vatican City, I am told that you are the most knowledgeable about the paranormal, and creatures such as myself."

Father Rovati said nothing, but continued to glare at Alec.

"The Book of Anu ... what do you know about it?" Alec asked.

"What interest would it be to you? It cannot change what you have become."

"I seek to end my curse, to live in the light," Alec confessed.

"As admirable as that goal is, it is also unrealistic." The priest's voice seemed to lose some of its sharp edge.

"I just want to find out what you know about it and where it can be found."

Father Rovati took a deep breath. "If it still exists, it is buried in the catacombs beneath Rome."

"But it *did* exist?" Alec felt his excitement grow.

The priest nodded. "It did ... yes."

"What is in the book?"

"Blasphemy! That is what is in the book. It will not help you achieve your goal."

"It reveals the truth of the vampire. I know that much. Tell me, what is in the book about my kind?" Alec pressed.

Father Rovati shook his head. "That you are not human. That the vampire is an abomination."

Alec's features were impassive. "I already know that much."

"Then you know all there is to know." The priest turned to walk away.

Alec would have stopped the man, but something told him he would get no more information. He was once again on his own, but this time he at least had some idea of where to look.

Leaving St. Peter's Square, Alec headed toward the underground cities of the dead. Now he would search in the catacombs.

His thoughts strayed to Nicole and he pulled his mobile phone from his pocket. He'd not phoned her since leaving New Orleans, and at that moment, every fiber of his being longed to hear her voice.

His main purpose for leaving had been to search for the Book of Anu, but it had also been to give her some space. He wanted her to have time to decide if loving an immortal was something that she really wanted.

Alec put the phone back in his pocket. He would call her soon, but now was not the right time.

Losing himself in thought dulled his senses. Alec did not notice the shadowy figure that followed him from the square, or how the figure was gaining on him.

Chapter Eleven

The constant tap - tap of water did little to improve Darrien's mood. The dripping water annoyed him, but it was not the only thing keeping him from sleep. His accommodations were not luxurious by any stretch of the imagination, but the sea cave kept him from the sun, and the natural pools of water were ideal for bathing. He could hunt at night, and easily return to the cave before sunrise. Best of all, it was close to Sarah.

But now something was different. There had been a change in the vibes he was picking up from her thoughts. Throughout the day he had felt her despair - her pain, but now he felt a buzz of excitement coming from her. If it were not for the sun that still hung in the western horizon, Darrien would have left his dark haven. He would assure himself that she was okay. But that was not possible - he was a prisoner of the night. Only in the dark could he move about - only then could he offer her the protection that she needed.

Darrien closed his eyes so that he could retreat into himself. The shame that was working its way into his brain was as tormenting as knowing what he'd done to her when she was Caroline. Last time he'd let her die, this time he had taken her soul from the light.

How had it happened?

He'd been so careful to keep from infecting her, but still she had been overtaken by the hunger.

Darrien trembled at the memory of her soft skin and the moist heat of her womanhood. Oh how he'd wanted to take her - sate his hunger with her willing body and quench his thirst with her warm blood. He'd wanted Sarah more than he'd ever wanted anything, but his need to protect her overcame his need to possess her.

He'd mistakenly called her by her former name. Why had he called her Caroline when he knew she didn't believe? Even now he could feel her pain and knew how he had gashed at her heart when he'd uttered Caroline's name.

The urge to go to her was unbelievable, but he kept reminding himself that even if he could leave the cave, he could not let himself approach her again. If he was mistaken and she had not yet turned, then being near her was too risky.

* * * *

Closing her eyes, Sarah let the spray of hot water wash away her tension and the grime that had accumulated on her body while she'd held up in the basement. Her mind drifted to the lycan. He wanted to take her away from Sutter Point. Though her sixth sense told her that she could trust him, Sarah could not help but feel that she was moving toward disaster.

"Go now." The voice was distant and the words muffled.

At first she wasn't sure she'd heard anything at all, or even what the person was saying, but then she heard the voice again.

"Go now."

This time the words were unmistakable. It was a girl's voice.

Sarah quickly rinsed the rest of the soap from her body and turned off the water, hoping that she would hear more. After drying herself with the towel, she stepped over to the fogged mirror and wiped the moisture from the glass.

Gasping, Sarah swung around to see if the image that she saw in the mirror was actually standing behind her, but the room was empty. When she turned back to face the mirror, Gina was still there, staring at her with those dark - angry eyes.

Sarah began to shake. All of the terror of that horrible night came back, and with it, the guilt for not being able to find a way to stop what she'd known would happen. She may not have known the specifics, but she had known something would happen.

"I'm so sorry," Sarah cried.

Gina shook her head. "Go now."

Sarah could not pick up the sound of Gina's voice, but she read her friend's lips. It was as if the harder Sarah tried to hear her, the less sensitive she was to Gina's presence.

And then Gina was gone.

Still shaking, Sarah went to her room to dress. So many people were telling her to leave that it would be foolish to ignore the warnings any longer. Last night she'd been attacked by one of Omar's vamps, but Darrien had shown up in time to intervene. The next time he may not be there to save her.

Her adept fingers began weaving her long - auburn hair into a single braid. It was not the most stylish way to do her hair, but sufficient for travel, which is what she suspected she'd be doing soon.

What about Darrien?

She'd told him to leave her alone, but now she realized that the thought of never seeing him again was too painful.

Already she felt her heart growing heavy at the thought of leaving Sutter Point without saying goodbye. She had no idea where Darrien stayed during the day, or how she could get a message to him to let him know she was leaving.

As Sarah stood in front of the mirror, the young woman that stared back at her appeared so normal - so middle of the road American. Why is it that she felt so bizarre - like some type of sideshow freak?

A male voice from behind caught her attention. "You are missing him?"

She could see no one reflected in the mirror, but when she turned, Sarah saw Zaltar reclined on her bed. She quickly turned back to the mirror, but his reflection was not there.

There was deep laughter. "You will not see me in the mirror. I have no human soul. My life energy is on a higher vibration than what exists in this dimension."

"Why are you here? I didn't summons you."

"I am here to help my lady with her pain." As the words came from his mouth, Zaltar changed, becoming Darrien.

"Come ... let me relieve your suffering," he said, patting the area of the bed next to where he lay.

Sarah reddened. Zaltar wanted to make love to her while he imitated Darrien. He wanted this because that is what he believed she wanted. She was ready to reprimand him for showing up without being called, but then she remembered that he'd helped to save her life the night before, by doing exactly that.

Sarah shook her head. "Thanks for the offer, but I really need it to be Darrien." As she said those words she realized that it was true. No one made her feel the way he did. It had to be him.

"Sarah," Jeanie called from the bottom of the stairs. "Dinner is ready."

Sarah left her room and hurried to the kitchen. Their guest was already seated at the table and Jeanie was serving roast beef and gravy, with mashed potatoes and carrots. Her Aunt Jeanie never failed to amaze her. No matter what was going on, she could still whip up a great meal.

The whole time she'd been upstairs, Sarah had dreaded the idea of discussing her situation with the stranger. However, as soon as she resigned herself to her situation, she began to feel a certain amount of excitement at the prospect of setting off on a new adventure. It would be a new chapter in her life. She was sure that was what it would end up being. When she left Sutter Point this time, she would be entering a different phase in her life.

Sarah had better manners than to approach the subject while they were eating, but she could hardly contain herself until the meal was over.

"Where are you taking me?" she asked.

Lex smiled, apparently pleased with her eagerness to talk. "Your aunt tells me that you have been attending college," he said, avoiding a direct answer.

Sarah nodded. "I've been going to the university in Portland, but came home for the summer."

"Well ... would you mind maybe taking a few summer classes?" he asked.

Sarah shrugged. "I guess not. Is that the plan ... to send me back to Portland?"

Lex shook his head. "That would never work. If they have tracked you here, they likely know that you have been going to school in Portland."

"Then what?"

"There is a girl I know who is going to school in another part of the country. She is the daughter of a lycan, but she does not possess the ability to change. I have spoken with her and she thinks it would be a great idea if you come and stay with her for a time."

"How would I be safe there? Especially if this girl cannot change, as you say." Sarah was doubtful that Lex's solution was any solution at all. She would probably be safer if she stayed with Darrien.

"Because no one can know where you are ... not your aunt, your friends, no one. Omar will not have any idea of where to find you," Lex reasoned. "Furthermore, from what I gather from your aunt, the two of you have quite a lot in common."

"What do you mean that my aunt cannot know where I'm going?" Sarah didn't like this idea at all. If this man turned out to be an enemy, she would be at his mercy.

"The vampire can probe the minds of some people," Lex explained. "They will try to discover where you've gone by doing this with the people closest to you."

"Well I don't like the idea of leaving my aunt alone here, especially if there is any chance that she may become the target of these vampires," Sarah told him, stubbornly folding her arms in front of her.

Jeanie smiled and that spark of good humor danced in her eyes. "Oh Sarah sweetheart, your old auntie is quite capable of taking care of herself. It is you that we must worry about."

Sarah was not so sure that Jeanie could hold her own against these vampires. They were so much more powerful than what she'd ever imagined. "For how long?" she wanted to know.

"I hope that it will not be long." Lex stood from the table and looked over at Jeanie. "This was the best meal I've eaten in years. Thank you so much Miss Fabre."

Jeanie was beaming. Sarah got the distinct impression that her aunt had more than a passing interest in the lycan.

When can you be ready to travel?" Lex turned his attention to Sarah. "I want to be gone before the sun goes down."

"What about you?" Sarah asked her aunt.

"I will go stay with a friend for a few days. By then they will have realized that you are no longer in the area."

"Well it sounds like the two of you have already worked out all of the details. You promised to tell me why I crave blood," Sarah frowned.

"We have a long drive ahead of us. There will be plenty of time to talk. I know this may seem extreme to you right now, but you will be much safer," Lex assured her.

Sarah could not help but wonder.

Chapter Twelve

The dark was full of the sounds of night creatures, and though Nicole should have found comfort in the tranquility of their presence, the hooting of owls and the chirping of crickets made her feel a little edgy. They stood in the same derelict cemetery where Alec had been only days before. Just like Alec, they stared up at the ancient castle.

"That's a long climb," she said, looking over at Dash.

Dash shrugged his shoulders. "Don't be silly. We'll just sail right up there."

"You know, I've been meaning to ask … how do you do that? How do you fly?"

"Have you ever heard of telekinesis?" he asked, running a hand across the skin on his head, as if he were feeling for hair that was not there.

Nicole nodded.

"Well it's like that. Only with the vampire, the power is magnified thousands of times. The part of the brain that controls telekinesis is enhanced by the mutation during the changing." Dash explained patiently.

Nicole smiled, happy that he was finally talking. Dash had been unusually quiet during the trip. She'd taken it for disappointment that Sophia had decided not to join them, but now she wondered. It just didn't seem as if he'd been very close with the female vampire, and it wasn't like Dash to be so quiet.

"What's bothering you?" she asked. Nicole wanted to know that her friend was okay before they went any further.

"What makes you think there's something wrong?" Dash frowned.

"I know you Dash, and I can tell when something is wrong."

Giving Nicole a lopsided grin, Dash pulled something from his pocket and handed it to her. It was a folded piece of paper.

Nicole unfolded the paper, but couldn't really make out what was on it. "What is it?" she asked.

Dash handed her a tiny flashlight that he'd pulled out of his other pocket. "Brought this just for you," he told her.

"Thanks," she said, taking the flashlight.

When Nicole switched the light on and directed the beam onto the paper, she saw that it was a picture of a beach, probably somewhere in the Caribbean. "This is a nice picture."

"Sometimes I close my eyes and imagine that I am sleeping on that beach. Feeling the warmth of the sun."

Dash stared up at the castle.

"I will never go to a place like that … will I? At least not in the daylight." Dash turned his attention back to Nicole.

Nicole placed a hand gently on his arm. "If there is a way for you to live in the light … we'll find it," she promised.

Dash was still staring up at the dark structure. As Nicole peered at the Castle Arges, a feeling of foreboding tugged at her senses.

"Well let's go," he told Nicole. Wrapping his arms around her waist, Dash carried her with him as he flew to the top of the cliffs.

They came down in an overgrown garden at the front of the castle. It looked as if no one had bothered to care for the garden and lawns of the castle for years.

"Appears as if they need a gardener," Dash said, poking Nicole in the ribs.

"Ouch!" Nicole glared at him.

"Sorry,' he smiled. "Just knew that's what you were thinking."

"Really?"

Dash nodded and started walking around the exterior of the castle.

"What are you doing?"

"Well I'm looking for a way in … what do you think?" Dash scowled.

"I thought we'd just knock on the door."

He stared at her as if she were a creature from another planet. "You can't be serious?"

"Well yeah … actually. It just seems the right way to do it. After all, we really don't want to put this guy in a bad mood right from the beginning," Nicole told him as she started for the gatehouse, and the entrance to the outer courtyard of the castle.

"What do you think? That he's going to ask you in for a spot of tea?" Dash asked as he started after her.

"Maybe." Nicole threw him a smile.

Dash shook his head. "You are nuttier than a fruitcake."

Nicole ignored the comment and continued to make her way through the weeds to the gatehouse. The tall wrought iron gate that led to the outer courtyard was not shut and locked, like she thought it would be. But then again, it was not as if anyone local would dare to trespass at Castle Arges.

Once inside the courtyard, she could see the main entrance to the castle. On each side of the large double doors were stone - carved gargoyles. The grotesque creatures added to the macabre atmosphere of the castle. Though they had probably stood in the same place for hundreds of years, Nicole thought they were an appropriate addition to the residence of a vampire like Luciano. He was not just one of the ancients, but a vampire that was far more powerful than the mythical Dracula. Luciano could have been Dracula, if such a character had ever really existed. Nicole didn't know a lot about him, but she did know that he was both feared and respected by the other vampires.

On each of the thick - wooden doors was a brass knocker. Without hesitating, Nicole clasped the cold metal in her hand and pounded on the door several times. Dash stood behind her. She could sense that he was ready to flee, but to his credit he stood his ground, knowing that she might need his help.

After several moments no one had come to the door so Nicole knocked again. Before she could pull her hand away from the knocker, the door swung open. The small woman could have been no more than five feet tall. She was old. Nicole guessed the woman to be at least in her seventies. She wore a black maid's dress and a white cap on her head. It was not a uniform that you would expect to see on a house servant in the twenty-first century.

The old lady stared at them like she was not quite sure they were real.

"We've come to see Luciano. Is he in?" Nicole asked.

The woman continued to stare silently.

"Madam?" Nicole prodded.

"You must be mad to come here … when you are not one of them." She spoke in heavily accented English. As the woman spoke the last word, she stared directly at Dash. It was obvious that she could tell which of them was a vampire.

Nicole could not help but wonder why a human would be in the employ of a vampire like Luciano, someone that avoided contact with people as much as possible.

Nicole smiled. "It is very important that I speak with him."

The old lady nodded and stepped aside so that they could enter. She motioned to a door at the left of the entry hall. "Wait in there and I will tell him you are here. Who shall I say you are?"

"My name is Nicole Ashe." Nicole paused when she saw that Dash was shaking his head. For some reason he didn't want her to reveal her name. Ignoring him, Nicole continued. "I'm Donavan Ashe's daughter."

When the woman left the room, Dash turned on her. "Are you crazy? Have you forgotten that a born vampire is forbidden?"

Nicole shook her head. "No I haven't forgotten. But if we are to expect any cooperation, I have a feeling we are going to have to be upfront with this vampire. Besides…chances are he would be able to sense what I was anyway."

"The young lady would be correct." The deep - soothing voice seemed to come out of nowhere.

Nicole's eyes scanned the room, but at first she didn't see him - not until he moved. There was a figure standing at the large window that looked out onto the dark courtyard. Dash was standing near Nicole, his mouth agape with surprise. Considering Dash was a vampire, Nicole had to assume that this was extraordinary, even for an immortal. Luciano had moved so quickly that they had not been aware that he'd entered the room. She was positive the room had been empty when they'd walked in.

Nicole had to catch her breath when she looked at him. He was too perfect to be real. If her heart had not already belonged to another, she could see how it would be too easy to fall under Luciano's spell.

The vampire's black hair was long and silky, falling to his waist. His eyes were almost completely black, but with the glowing light of the immortal. His features were soft, but masculine at the same time.

"Lord Luciano," Nicole said, nodding her head.

"And you would be the daughter of my old friend, Donavan?" Luciano stepped away from the window and closer to them.

Nicole nodded. "I have come to locate a friend that traveled here a couple of weeks ago."

"Would that happen to be Alec Norwood?" Luciano gave her a dark smile.

"Yes, that's him. Has he been here?" Nicole asked, her composure cracking slightly.

"He was here. He invaded my home without the benefit of an invitation." Luciano's eyes sparked with anger.

"Is he still here?" Nicole asked, holding her breath. She was happy to finally get some information about Alec's whereabouts, but terrified of what might have happened to him for angering Luciano.

Luciano eyed her curiously. "Interesting that a mortal would worry so much about a vampire's fate. But then again Miss Ashe … you are not a mere mortal, are you?"

Dash cleared his throat. "Lord Luciano, Miss Ashe is Donavan's daughter, so you know what that makes her. We beg that your grace not punish her for the sins of her father."

Luciano smiled. "What an absurd assumption. In a way Miss Ashe is no different than myself. She was born to be what she is."

Though Luciano seemed to be reasonable, Nicole was guarded. "And Alec ... what happened to him?"

"Oh yes ... Alec, your ... lover." Luciano looked into her eyes, reading her as if she were an open book.

Now Nicole knew he was no ordinary vampire. He could read her far too easily. Probing her thoughts was as effortless for this immortal as pulling files from a cabinet.

Luciano continued. "He came here to search for the Book of Anu. I simply told him it was not here, and where he might find it."

"Where is that?" Nicole asked.

"The holy city of course. Where else would the humans hide such a hideous reminder of the immortal?"

Nicole was confused and it showed on her face.

"Rome ... Vatican City," Dash explained.

Nicole sighed. It would seem that their journey had just begun. Fear gnawed at her stomach. Somehow she knew that Alec was in danger, even if it had nothing to do with Luciano.

* * * *

The house stood silent and dark. For a long time Darrien continued to gaze at Sarah's home, as if he could not quite believe that no one was there. She was gone! He could no longer feel her presence. It was not like she had just gone into town, or was out on some errand. She was truly gone. If she'd been anywhere near, he would have been able to feel her.

Sarah had left without so much as a word to him!

But wasn't that what he'd wanted her to do? He told her many times that she was not safe in Sutter Point, and that she should leave. She'd finally taken his advice, but he'd thought, or at least hoped that she would say goodbye.

Sarah was gone and the Fabre house was empty, but still something wasn't right. Slowly, Darrien moved closer to the house. As he approached the front door, he felt sorrow seep into his heart. The door stood open, hanging from one hinge. The wood frame around the door was splintered. Pieces of it lay scattered on the porch.

They had been there for her, but how? He'd come to her house as soon as the sun had gone down. How had they had enough time to get to her before he had? Unless they'd been hiding someplace close, waiting for night.

Darrien stepped inside. It was dark, but he could see through the darkness. The house was trashed. Pictures had been pulled from the walls, the curtains hung in shreds around the windows, and furniture had been turned over.

Omar's followers were not the most sophisticated of hunters. They tended to leave destruction in their wake. This was how he knew that the intruders had been Omar's vamps. Had they gotten her or had she been able to get away?

Darrien cursed himself for not being able to get there sooner. There was no blood. He had to assume that she'd escaped, but the aunt was gone also.

How would he ever find her? And find her was something that he knew he must do. She was his life, the only source of light for his soul. Without her, the last spark of humanity that burned within his heart would soon succumb to the darkness. He had to know that she was safe.

* * * *

Sarah blinked and opened her eyes just as the lights of Reno came into view. The last thing she remembered before dozing off was leaving Sacramento and heading toward Donner Pass. She must have slept right through Lake Tahoe.

Having little opportunity to travel while she was growing up, Sarah found the trip exciting. At least it was exciting as long as she could forget why she was taking the trip, and as long as she didn't think about Darrien. He would never know what happened to her. That thought brought on an ache in her chest and a feeling of emptiness.

"I hear the University of Nevada is a fine school," Lex commented when he saw her peering curiously out the window as they drove by the campus.

"At least I'll be able to keep busy."

The two traveling companions said no more. Both Sarah and Lex were content to let the silence settled between them. At the beginning of the trip there had been a lot of conversation. Sarah had a great deal that she wanted to know, but now she preferred to retreat into herself.

Sarah now understood that her craving for blood was something that was bred into her. It would never go away. As soon as she'd caught the scent of Darrien's blood, that hunger had awakened in her. Now it would be with her the rest of her life. It was just one of the consequences of being a born vampire. Not all born vampires had the craving, but she did. Something else that she'd found out from Lex was that she was probably immune to the poison of the vampire. Even if she were bitten, and fed on the blood of a vampire, she most likely wouldn't turn.

According to Lex, this was a strength that she should appreciate. It would be especially useful if Omar were to ever get the idea to turn her, as he had apparently tried to do to her older sister. Sarah was extremely curious about these sisters, but Lex had refused to give her their names, at least not yet. He feared she might try to find them on her own, and put all of them in danger.

Lex turned off of the highway and into an apartment complex located close to the campus.

"So who is it that I will be staying with exactly, and does she know what I am?" Sarah was becoming a little apprehensive about staying with someone she didn't even know.

"Well ... you could say that she is the daughter of an old family friend. My daughter is married to her father's cousin. There are some things about her and where she comes from that she has been instructed not to reveal. In fact, she can't talk about this. It is against the laws of her people. She doesn't know a lot about you, except that you are in danger. I did tell her about your gift." Lex forced a smile.

Sarah was no longer sure she'd made the right decision. Lex still seemed a little apprehensive, and this made her nervous. She wanted to hit him with a storm of questions, but instead she asked, "What's her name?"

"Summer Gray Eagle. Like I said, the two of you will have a lot in common."

Sarah couldn't quite understand what they could have in common. This Summer Gray Eagle was the daughter of a lycan, while she was the daughter of a vampire.

When they had parked, Lex popped the trunk open so that they could grab Sarah's luggage. With both of them carrying bags, Sarah followed him up a staircase to the top floor of one of the buildings. Lex tapped on the door.

Sarah held her breath, waiting for the door to open. She wasn't sure what it was that she expected to see - maybe a girl with hair all over her and big teeth? When the door swung open, Sarah was actually surprised to see a striking young woman staring back at them.

"Hello," the girl said, as she stepped aside and let them enter.

Sarah was in awe of the girl's stunning beauty. She had a tan complexion that appeared to be completely natural. Sarah would have killed to have the girl's long golden-brown hair. Summer had the most exotic golden eyes Sarah had ever seen. They were like the eyes of a cat.

"This is Sarah," Lex told the girl.

"Hi," she said with a smile, holding out her hand to take Sarah's. "I'm Summer."

Feeling a little unsure of herself, Sarah forced a smile to her lips and nodded to acknowledge Summer's greeting.

"I'll show Sarah to her room and then make us some refreshments," Summer told Lex.

Lex shook his head. "That's not necessary. I must be on my way, and the two of you will probably want to get to know each other."

"Are you sure?" Summer obviously didn't like the idea of sending her guest away without refreshments.

"Yes," Lex smiled. "I'll be in touch soon."

Lex was gone, and Sarah was left alone with the lycan's daughter.

Summer picked up a couple of bags and motioned for Sarah to follow her.

"I hope you like your room," Summer told her. "It's the room that my roommate uses, but Penny's gone home for a few months."

"Oh, will she mind if I'm using her room?"

Summer shook her head. "No ... she won't be back for awhile anyway."

"I really appreciate this. I don't know how to thank you." Sarah set her bags down in the small room. On the twin bed was a comforter, decorated with a spray of brightly colored flowers. Against the opposite wall there was a small dresser and a little mirror. It wasn't a luxury hotel, but it was nice.

"I'll let you get settled in and then we can have a cup of coffee, if you'd like?" Summer offered.

"Yes, that would be nice."

Summer left the room, shutting the door behind her. Sarah decided she liked the girl. She hadn't picked up any negative vibes from her at all. In fact, Sarah was getting the impression that Summer was glad for the company.

Chapter Thirteen

Alec easily gained entry to the ancient church that was also the entryway to the Catacombs of St. Domitilla. It was one of the largest of Rome's catacombs, consisting of miles of tunnels and four layers. The Catacombs of St. Domitilla were also among the oldest. If the Church was keeping the Book of Anu, it made sense that they might hide it in such a place.

The staircase leading to the tombs started out okay, but it soon changed, running into the original staircase. Alec assumed that the book would be hidden among the Christian burials, maybe even one that had been ordained a saint.

In the dark, there was no way to detect the predator that was behind him, but Alec's sensed a presence. Stopping, he spun around to see who had followed him into the catacombs. Before he could react, he was slammed in the head with a blunt object and sent flying down the stairs.

The blow had stunned him, but not to the point that he could not act. Alec was on his feet, his eyes glowing with anger. He drew back his lips to reveal his sharp - white fangs. The dark figure flew toward him, but Alec easily maneuvered out of the way. Again his attacker swung at him with what appeared to be a large stick, but this time Alec was able to avoid being hit.

Now his pursuer pulled out a gun. But instead of feeling the separation of flesh like he expected to feel when he heard the blast, the gun was silent. All he felt was a sharp prick in his leg. He had barely enough time to realize that he'd been tranquilized before blacking out.

* * * *

Sarah left her bedroom to join her new roommate. When she entered the living room, her eyes caught movement in a dark corner. There were two lamps to illuminate the room, but the lighting was dim, leaving the corners of the room in shadow. Gina stared at her from the darkness.

Sarah knew that she should not fear her friend, but the grotesque image left her trembling.

"Go away now," Sarah whispered, hoping that she could urge Gina to go into the light. Why was she still hanging around, Sarah had left Sutter Point like her friend wanted.

"Is that you Sarah?" Summer called from the kitchen.

"Yes," Sarah spoke up.

"The coffee is ready," Summer told her.

Turning her back on the horrifying image of her friend, Sarah stepped into the kitchen. On the table were two cups of coffee, and sweet rolls.

"I wasn't sure if you'd had time to eat on your trip here. I thought you might be hungry."

"Thanks," Sarah smiled.

"So that girl in the living room ... do you know why she's here?" Summer asked casually.

Sarah stared at the other woman. "You can see her?"

Summer nodded. I can see the dead. A gift I inherited from my mother, though she is a lot better at it than I am."

"So that's why Lex said we would have a lot in common?" Sarah finally saw some of the pieces starting to fit together.

"Yes, he told me that you could do this. He also thought you might need some help in coping with your gift."

Sarah shook her head. "My Aunt Jeanie can be such a busybody sometimes."

Summer laughed. "I know the feeling. I have a few relatives like that myself."

The smile on Sarah's face vanished. "I don't know why she's here. She was warning me to leave, back when I was in Sutter Point. But she's still around so I don't know."

"Well, have you asked her why she's here?" Summer placed a large cinnamon roll on Sarah's plate.

"Not really,'

"Why don't we go find out what she wants then?"

"Okay, I guess it couldn't hurt." Sarah smiled and got up from her seat to follow Summer into the living room.

Gina was still in the same place that she'd been a few moments before. "They like corners for some reason," Summer informed her.

"How much do you know about ghosts?" Sarah asked. Though she herself should have been an expert after growing up with them, she had to admit that she didn't know that much about the otherworldly specters. She'd tried to avoid encounters with them as much as possible.

"I work with the local police to help solve missing persons cases and homicides, so I know a little," Summer admitted.

Sarah scrunched up her face. "That must be a frightening job? Facing death all of the time."

"I only do it part time. I'm still in school," Summer told her.

Gina hovered in the corner, but Sarah could not tell if her friend's ghost was even aware of their presence.

"What's her name?"

"Gina," Sarah answered in a low voice.

Summer moved slowly toward the corner where Gina hovered. "Gina … do you need something?" Her voice was gentle and even.

At first there was no response, but then the specter's eyes fixed on Sarah. "I'm waiting for Sarah. She has to listen to me."

Sarah's face turned white.

"What do you mean?" Summer's voice shook as she tried to get the spirit to reveal more.

"Death is near you Sarah," Gina's hollow voice drifted through the room and then she disappeared.

Sarah was shaking. She'd just been warned of impending death. She felt Summer's hand on her shoulder.

"Don't take too much notice of that," she tried to calm Sarah's fears.

"What do you mean? She practically told me that I'm going to die soon."

Summer shook her head. "Sometimes they get confused, or they talk in riddles." Despite her words, Summer looked worried.

"Let's go have our coffee now. I think she's gone for the moment."

Sarah nodded but said nothing.

"Maybe you can tell me what happened to her," Summer suggested.

Sarah wanted a friend. No, she needed a friend to talk with. But she still wasn't sure how much she could trust Summer.

If only she could tell someone about her dreams, about her need to see Darrien again - a vampire that had been ready to kill her.

* * * *

Darrien boarded the flight to New Orleans. When he stepped onboard the 747, he saw that his assigned seat was right next to Jeanie Fabre. It was just as he knew it would be. It had taken some effort to find Sarah's aunt, but he'd finally located her at a small cottage in the woods.

He hadn't approached her then. He'd sensed the intense suspicion of the witches she was with. The last thing he needed right now was to do battle with some overzealous witches. His time would be better spent searching for Sarah.

Instead, Darrien had watched Jeanie, waiting for the perfect time to talk with her. But the witch had not been left alone for even a moment. Then he'd followed her to the airport in Portland where Jeanie had bought a ticket to New Orleans. Darrien used his charm and power of persuasion to convince the girl at the ticket counter to assign him a seat next to Jeanie.

Jeanie wouldn't exactly be alone, but at least she seemed to be the only witch onboard.

When Darrien took the seat next to Jeanie, the witch turned her hard green eyes on him. "What are you doing here?"

"I'm looking for Sarah. Where has she gone?"

Jeanie shrugged her shoulders. "She has gone underground, and I was not informed where she would be."

"Why are you going to New Orleans then?" The corners of his lips lifted into a smile.

"Personal business," Jeanie glared.

"I see," Darrien said, reaching out to pull a magazine from the pouch that was attached to the chair in front of him. He began flipping through the pages, but without paying any attention to what he was looking at.

"You do realize that she is in danger, and very likely unprotected at this moment." Darrien continued.

"She has plenty of protection," Jeanie told him.

"I doubt it."

Jeanie leaned closer so that she could whisper. "A lycan took her away."

Darrien fixed angry eyes on her. "You actually let her go with one of those beasts?"

Jeanie waved her hand, dismissing his words. "Just prejudice, that's all."

"Are you kidding? The wolves are enemies! They will kill her if they haven't already." Darrien raised his voice in anger.

"Well she isn't a vampire. No thanks to you,' Jeanie told him in a low voice.

Darrien was visibly relieved.

A small blond girl popped her head over the chair in front of them.

"Keep your voice down," Jeanie whispered.

The girl smiled at them and then turned to talk to someone in the seat next to her. "Hey daddy! There are vampires behind us."

"Sit down and stop being rude." The father chastised the child.

Jeanie giggled. "How do you avoid vampire slayers with such carelessness?"

"I don't usually get this angry," he sighed. "So who is this wolf and what does he want with Sarah?"

"Well not that it's any of your business," Jeanie reminded him, "but he works with the Light Seekers."

Darrien rolled his eyes. "That crazy bunch."

"I think they're onto something."

Darrien said nothing. What could he say? The Light Seekers were responsible for spreading false hope. They were dreamers, and would always be chasing something that they would probably never find.

"So tell me. Why so much interest in my niece? You were going to kill her anyway?" Jeanie asked.

He struggled to find the right words, but finally he decided it was best to say it as simply as he could. "I love her," he told the witch.

The expression on Jeanie's face turned serious. "You know, the love of an immortal destroyed my sister ... Sarah's mother?"

Darrien turned away. "That doesn't change what is true."

"What could you offer her but a life of darkness? Children that would hunger for blood?"

"I just want to be sure that she gets through this okay," he told Sarah's aunt.

"Hmm ... and you don't think that the more she is with you, the worse it's going to hurt her when you are gone?"

Darrien had no answer for her. It was all he could do to keep his hands off of Sarah when she was near. How could he be sure that he would not pull her further into the despair of his love?

Closing his eyes, Darrien let his thoughts wander to that long ago night. Even now that he'd found her again, the pain still tore at his soul. He could almost taste her lips - feel her soft mounds of flesh in his hands. He loved the way her perky brown buds hardened at his touch, and how she'd gasp when he pinched them.

Drifting into sleep, Darrien dreamt of the witch that was his soul mate.

"Caroline ... please! I must have you again. I cannot rest until I do.

She smiled. "My, your appetites are no different than when you were a man."

"I am far more ravenous now," he said, gathering her in his arms.

Caroline struggled, but only halfheartedly. When his mouth came down on hers, she parted her lips to accept his probing tongue. The more he tasted the warmth of her mouth, the more he wanted her.

He had to have her then, even if she protested.

Darrien lifted Caroline into his arms and carried her to the feather bed near the fireplace. After laying her gently on the bed, he began unbuttoning her dress. Slowly at first, but his hunger drove him to madness and he ripped the remaining cloth from her body.

"We can't *chéri*," Caroline whispered. "You killed my husband."

"I should have been your husband," he told her, licking at her budding nipples.

And then there were no more words. She offered herself to him completely. Just as he joined with her, the door to the cottage flew open. An angry crowd stood at the door, their torches bathing the naked couple in revealing light.

"The witch has taken the devil to her bed!" someone screamed.

Darrien flew at the crowd, but there were just too many of them. He felt the flame of the torch ignite his hair, and then he was ablaze, his body melting away. Rolling onto the ground, he eventually put the fire out, but he had already received grave injuries. He was too weak to help protect her.

For years he'd been haunted by the sound of her screams as they drug her away. Though he'd not healed completely, within a few hours he'd been strong enough to go to her, but he'd only had moments until sunrise. They'd taken her to a local jail where she'd received a mock trial before she burned.

The witch trials had been over for two hundred years. But in such a religious parish, they would still burn witches in secret.

Darrien stood outside of the barred window and called to her. "Caroline."

He heard movement from inside, and then he heard her voice. "You still live *monsieur?*"

"Yes, but I am still recovering. Let me take you out of there. Let me turn you so that you no longer have to worry about this."

For several moments she said nothing. When she finally did speak, she did not say the words that he'd hoped to hear. "I will suffer my fate my lord. If I try to cheat death, it will come to my child. I ask only that you do something for me. Please take my daughter to the Coven of Lazar? They will care for her."

"But Caroline my love, I cannot let you go to your death!"

"You must! Now go Darrien. The sun is almost up."

For the first time since he'd turned, he felt a tear slip down his cheek. "I love you," he told her.

"And I love you. It was always you my lord."

"I cannot go on without you,' he told her, his voice quivering with pent up emotion.

"I will return to you someday," she promised. "You will know it is me when you look into my eyes."

He'd left her then - left her to a fate that she had not deserved. The plague had taken the lives of many of the locals, and they had to blame someone. Naturally it had to be the witch that slept with the devil. Never mind the fact that it was Caroline that had actually nursed many of those that had survived the plague.

Bitterness burned within Darrien's heart. He could barely endure thinking about what they'd done to her. The next night they'd taken her deep into the swamps and burned her. They would have killed the child too, if Darrien had not taken her away before the townspeople could find her.

Darrien jumped awake when he felt a sharp pain in his side. Opening his eyes, he saw Jeanie staring at him, ready to poke him with her finger again.

"We are getting ready to land," she informed him. "I didn't think vampires slept so soundly," she added.

Darrien said nothing, but gave her a sour look.

A perky blond flight attendant leaned down and whispered in his ear. "Sir ... you must fasten your seat belt."

When Darrien fastened his belt, the woman moved down the aisle to the next rebellious passenger.

"I don't need this thing," Darrien muttered, his mood dark after reliving Caroline's death through his dream.

"You could at least pretend," Jeanie scowled.

Chapter Fourteen

Alec swallowed hard. It felt as if his skin was on fire. His body was so weak from not feeding that he could barely move. His mind filled with images of blood - blood gushing into his mouth as he bit into a beating artery - a soft neck. Saliva dripped from his mouth at the thought.

He was only lucid for moments at a time. Beyond that, everything was a blur. He remembered a sharp sting, and then he'd blacked out. It was dark - the air was cool and musky. He was sure he was somewhere within the catacombs, but he had no clue who his captor was, or for what purpose they were keeping him alive.

Someone stroked his face softly and he instinctively growled. "Oh Alec! I know you want to feed, but your dinner isn't here yet," the female voice cooed.

In the haze of his hunger, Alec struggled to place the voice. It was Julia. Somehow they'd tracked him to Rome.

"Bitch!" he snarled.

Her dark laughter enraged him and he struggled with the chains to break free.

Julia stepped closer, taking care to stay away from his fangs. He was suffering from blood deprivation, but he could still see her, though the image was dim.

"Alec, would you like to hear a secret?" Julia asked, her voice purring. "If you inject a vampire with liquid folic acid, it will drop his blood count instantly. It will render him unconscious? The vampire becomes blood deprived as soon as it goes through his system."

Again Alec growled and pulled on the chains. The rattling and clanking of the chains echoed through the tunnels of the catacomb.

"Don't fret dear. Your human bitch will be here to feed you soon," Julia laughed. "She really is a disobedient child … going against everything her father tells her."

Her last words reverberated through his head, gradually fading away as he slipped into blissful darkness.

* * * *

Jeanie stared down at the name of the coffee shop she'd scribbled on the notepaper. The Hole was on the first floor of the mall. An unlikely place to meet a vampire, but it was where Donavan had instructed her to be.

Darrien was still with her. She'd tried to talk him into waiting at the hotel, but he wasn't having it. Jeanie had to admit that his concern for Sarah seemed genuine enough, but she was worried how Donavan might react to one of Omar's assassins showing up with her.

The two of them stood outside the coffee shop instead of waiting for Donavan inside. She wasn't sure what to expect, it had been years since she'd seen him, and even then she'd not been too cordial. As soon as Beth had told her about Donavan, she'd known that the vampire would eventually bring heartbreak into her sister's life, just like she suspected would happen with Sarah.

When Jeanie caught sight of him, she was struck with his dark charm, just like her sister must have been. He was tall, and his dark eyes spoke of mysteries better left to the imagination. Even though the style was outdated, he still wore his black hair long, as many vampires did.

As he rode the escalator from the second floor, his eyes strayed to the two people waiting in front of the coffee shop. Donavan stepped off of the escalator and started toward them.

"Miss Fabre," he nodded without acknowledging her companion.

"Donavan," Jeanie greeted him, but she could not force a smile.

"Would you care for some coffee?" he asked.

"Sure." Jeanie followed him into the dimly lit coffee shop. It was different than most cafes, which were usually illuminated with bright fluorescent lights. Jeanie knew that vampires had an aversion to bright lighting.

When they were settled into an isolated booth and had received their drinks, Donavan turned his attention to Jeanie. "I'm assuming this must be about my daughter, Sarah?"

Jeanie nodded. "She was forced into hiding because your brother sent assassins to kill her."

Donavan shook his head, a sadness entering his eyes. "This does not surprise me. Omar will not stop until he has his way … or he is dead."

"What do you plan to do about it?" Jeanie wanted to know.

Donavan was silent for a long time and then he asked, "Is she in imminent danger at the moment?"

Jeanie shrugged her shoulders. "I don't know. When she went into hiding, I was not told where she would be. A lycan took her away."

Donavan gave her a dark look. "That was not a good idea."

"As I told her," Darrien finally spoke up.

"And who are you?" Donavan asked. "I know you are an immortal, but what is your interest in my daughter?"

Darrien's eyes locked with Donavan's "My only interest my lord … is that she remain safe."

"Is that so?" Donavan smiled, anger radiating from his eyes. "I hope for your sake your words are true."

Jeanie jumped in quickly, hoping to diffuse the conversation before it turned bad. "Beth … where is she?"

Donavan looked at her sharply. "What do you mean, where is Beth?"

"Don't you know? She left years ago to find you," Jeanie told him.

Donavan closed his eyes, a look of defeat spread across his face. "Why didn't you come to me then?"

"I thought that she'd found you and … turned," she said, an expression of distaste twisting her features.

"I have not set eyes on her since I left," he told her.

If Beth wasn't with Donavan, what happened to her? It must be exactly as she suspected. Her sister found a vampire that would turn her.

"So you have had my daughter all of this time?" he asked.

Jeanie nodded, unsure how to react to the news that her sister didn't just abandon her daughter for this vampire, but was truly missing. There were just too many emotions hitting her all at once. She felt disbelief, horror, and even anger at Donavan for bringing such tragedy to her family.

"How would I go about finding my sister and protecting Sarah?" Jeanie asked, her voice trembling.

Donavan shook his head. "There is no telling what happened to Beth, particularly as she has been gone so long. Sarah must come home to New Orleans, where I can keep her safe from my brother."

"The lycan felt it would be better if she stayed away from New Orleans," Jeanie informed him.

"Well he is not her father … I am." Donavan's voice was hard and unyielding.

"But Sarah will be safer if they don't know where she is?" Jeanie was leery about bringing her niece to New Orleans, and into the midst of so many vampires.

"With the lycans, she is in danger of two enemies instead of just one," Donavan explained.

"And Beth?" Jeanie reminded him.

"Do you have a pen and paper?"

Jeanie pulled out her notebook and a pen, handing them to Donavan. He scrawled something on the paper and gave it back to her. "Ethan is a vampire, but he is also a private investigator. He can help you retrace Beth's movements after she left."

"That's it? That's all you can do to help find the woman that gave up everything for you?" Jeanie was furious.

Donavan lifted his hands in a gesture of helplessness. "My concern must be for my daughter at this time. Beth has been gone a long time. I suspect that you may not like what you find."

Jeanie narrowed her eyes. "Would you care to tell your daughter that, because I sure don't want to?"

"I will go in search of my daughter. When I've found Sarah, I will explain the situation," he assured her.

"My lord," Darrien interrupted. "I will go and bring her back for you."

"And why would you do that?" Donavan asked.

Darrien could not find the words to explain why it was so important to him to be near Sarah, and to know that she was safe.

"Let me say it for you," Donavan frowned. "You are in love with her."

Darrien looked down, unable to deny the truth of the ancient vampire's words.

"Catching the heart of the immortal seems to be a talent of my daughters," Donavan growled.

"I will protect her no matter the cost," Darrien promised.

"If I give you this responsibility, it would mean your end if something happened to her," Donavan reminded him.

"I know," Darrien said, his voice low and difficult to hear.

"Don't you think you should tell him everything?" Jeanie drew her brows together, unsure if she trusted Darrien with her niece's life.

Donavan stared at Darrien, waiting for the other vampire to say whatever it was that Jeanie was referring to.

"Omar sent me to Sutter Point to kill Sarah. I was her assassin," Darrien told him, and then waited for Donavan's fury.

"So tell me ... what changed your mind?" Donavan asked, his voice deceivingly calm.

"Sarah's soul is the soul of someone I knew a long time ago. She was, and is the woman I love. I could never hurt her."

Donavan smiled. "I cannot help but wonder what happened to this woman that you loved? What happened that she should perish to then be reborn as my daughter?"

Darrien said nothing. How could he tell Sarah's father that it had been his fault that Caroline died?

Donavan held up his hand. "Do not worry. I don't believe in such things, but as long as it keeps you from harming my daughter, you are welcome to believe it. Maybe you will actually find salvation in your belief?"

Jeanie wanted to defend the concept of reincarnation because she knew it to be real, but she didn't necessarily believe it to be the case with Sarah. Darrien had fallen in love with their ancestress, and saw similarities in Sarah. It was only natural that he would see similarities. After all, Sarah was descended from Caroline Fabre, as all Fabre witches were.

"You can both get started by contacting Ethan," Donavan told them.

* * * *

Lex enjoyed the cool night breeze that had finally brought some relief from the stifling heat of the day. Sitting back on the bench, he watched as a young couple strolled through the square.

Jackson Square was one of his favorite spots in New Orleans, and one that he visited often. It provided him a way to step back and watch the world around him. The people were interesting, but what was even more fascinating were all of the other creatures that you could spot while watching from the sidelines. The people went about their business completely oblivious of those creatures. They just didn't know how to spot them.

Just as Lex was ready to glance at his watch, he saw the vampire emerge from the shadows of the St. Louis Cathedral. If you knew what to look for, there was no mistaking Donavan for anything other than what he was. He was all that one might imagine a vampire to be.

Donavan made his way straight to where Lex was sitting.

"Please ... have a seat," Lex told him.

Donavan said nothing. He stared at Lex, his dark eyes cutting right through him.

"So how can I help you?" Lex asked.

"Where is my daughter?"

"She is safe for the time being," Lex told him.

"Sarah belongs with me."

"And then what? Will you kill your own brother to protect her … a girl that should never have been born? Will you go against your own species and the ancients to keep her safe?" Lex asked.

"If need be, yes!" Donavan glared at him.

"I don't believe that you would," Lex stated.

"Why do you think it is your place to interfere with the immortals?" Donavan's voice was even, but his fury shone through in his eyes.

"It's all about balance," Lex told him. "If it continues like it has, that balance will be thrown off. When that happens then we must go to war to protect what we have been charged with protecting."

Donavan stepped closer. "She belongs with her own kind. You are endangering anyone that is with her."

Lex said nothing.

"If you tell me where to find Sarah, I give you my word that she will be safe, and that I will stand against my own kind to keep the balance that you speak of. I know that you will need my support to accomplish this," Donavan added.

Lex eyed the vampire, wondering just how far he could be trusted.

* * * *

Leaning against the balcony railing, Sarah gazed up at the dark sky - losing herself in the beauty of the night. From where she stood, the lights of Reno did not obscure the stars. When she looked to her left, she could see the neon lights of the casinos that made up much of the city. The location was perfect really. She was close enough to the city for easy access, but far enough away that she could still enjoy the night sky.

Though she had not come to Reno under the best of circumstances, her situation had turned out better than what she had hoped. Summer was fun to be with, and she didn't seem the least concerned about Sarah's background. Inhaling deeply, she savored the scent of roses that clung to the cool night air. Vine roses climbed the balcony rails, adding color to the already lovely view from Summer's apartment.

Closing her eyes, Sarah's thoughts drifted to the one person she should not let herself think about. There hadn't been a single sign of Darrien since leaving Sutter Point, but what had she expected? It wasn't as if he would have the slightest idea where to find her. In fact, he wasn't supposed to know where to find her.

When she thought of Darrien, she could not help but remember back to that night in the hedge maze. She remembered how magical it had felt to be in his arms - to feel his touch and how easily he had brought her to a place of pure bliss. Never in her life had she felt as safe as she had in his arms.

But then there was the darkness that had crept up on her - the craving for his blood, and the fear that she had turned. The shadow of uncertainty still taunted her, while her heart continued to call out to him. She yearned for his nearness and the safety of his arms, but then there was Caroline. Could she live with his love for this witch that had lived so long ago?

"You are Caroline." A voice echoed in her head.

In her dreams she relived Caroline's horror and felt the utter hopelessness of loving an immortal. She felt the fierce need to protect her child, but was she remembering or simply picking up on Caroline's energy with her own psychic abilities?

How could she ever know for sure if she really was Caroline, or just a reflection of the witch?

Blinking rapidly, she tried to hold back the hot tears that stung her eyes. If only Darrien loved her and not someone that he wanted her to be. Sarah was pulled from her thoughts when Summer slid the glass door open and stuck her head out.

"Just wanted to let you know that I was home." The smile on Summer's face faded when she saw the tears in Sarah's eyes.

"Are you okay?" Summer asked, stepping out onto the balcony.

"Yes." Sarah tried to smile. "Just feeling sorry for myself."

"Well we all have a right to do that sometimes. Is there anything I can do?" Summer took a seat at the small patio table that sat in the middle of the balcony.

Sarah shook her head. "It's nothing that won't get better with time."

"It's a guy right? It's always a guy!" Summer frowned.

Sarah shrugged. "Yeah, but he's not just an ordinary guy. It's a lot more complicated than that."

"Isn't it always?" Summer grinned and stood up. "I'll get us a couple of sodas and you can tell me about it?"

A moment later, Summer returned with the sodas and took her seat. "So ... tell me, what is so special about this guy?"

"How much do you know about me?" Sarah asked.

"Well ... I know you are in trouble and that you are a friend of Lex's. I also know that your father is a member of the vampire race. But I have to tell you, I've never actually seen a vampire."

"Well you have now. In a way ... I'm a vampire," Sarah told her. "Darrien is a vampire. He was turned hundreds of years ago. He thinks I am the reincarnation of a witch that he loved back then."

"Are you?" Summer asked, before taking a drink of her soda.

Sarah shrugged her shoulders. "She is one of my ancestors. I've had dreams of her and what happened to her, but I don't know if it's just something I'm picking up from her spirit."

"And you want this guy to love you for you, and not because he thinks you're someone else?"

Sarah nodded.

"I know how you feel," Summer admitted. "There's this guy ... I think I fell in love with him years ago, when I was just a little girl. He doesn't know I'm alive ... he still thinks I'm a child."

For a time, Summer seemed to be lost in memory, but then she smiled. "You know, the two of us shouldn't be sitting here pouting about the men we can't have. We should be out having fun."

"Oh I don't know," Sarah said, shaking her head. "I've never been too good with the whole social scene."

"Nonsense!" Summer stood up. "It's too late tonight, but maybe we could hit the town tomorrow night. What do you say?"

A sly smile spread across Sarah's face. "On one condition. You let me try a spell first. One for me and one for you." Now that she had been initiated into the coven, she'd been anxious to try out a spell. Why not one that might help both of them?

"What kind of spell?"

"A spell to find true love," Sarah was already looking around for something she could use.

Summer laughed. "Okay. But if we do happen to find our true love, how will we know that they are not just bewitched?"

"The spell would bring our true loves to us, but it won't make them love us. That will be all up to us."

"Okay," Summer shrugged. "I guess it couldn't hurt. I sure need a way to open that man's eyes, or at least get him here so I have a chance to open them myself."

"And I need ..."

"For him to see Sarah as Sarah," Summer finished for her.

"Yes," Sarah smiled. "That's what I need."

"Okay ... let's do it."

"Do you mind if I pick a couple of your roses?" Sarah asked.

Summer shook her head. "No ... go ahead."

Sarah broke off two white roses and placed them side-by-side on the table. She then picked up one and placed it in the palm of her hand. Closing her eyes, she gently blew on the flower. Magically, each petal began to separate from the flower and float in the air, before drifting away into the night sky. Soon all of the petals were gone.

"What was that?" Summer was in awe at what she'd just witnessed.

"It's a spell. The flower petals will go in search of your true love."

"Oh." Despite the magic she'd just witnessed, there was still uncertainty in Summer's voice.

Sarah repeated the spell. This time she sent the petals into the wind to bring back *her* true love.

"I guess we'll put this to the test tomorrow night." Summer got up from her chair. "This should be interesting."

"It may not work right away," Sarah informed the other girl. "But it does work. I've seen my Aunt Jeanie do this hundreds of times for others."

"Mine has a long way to come, so it probably will be awhile for me," Summer frowned.

"Do you want to talk about it?" Sarah asked.

Summer shook her head. "No, you would never believe it, besides I can't talk about my home. That's what Lex told me."

Sarah frowned. "Why is it such a secret anyway?"

Summer made a face. "Old rules. It's been like this forever, but maybe one day."

"Yes ... maybe one day." Sarah agreed, but her thoughts were already miles away. She wondered where Darrien was at that moment.

Chapter Fifteen

Nicole peered into the thick darkness of the catacombs, but she couldn't see a thing. Once again she cursed the human weakness that kept her from seeing in the dark. Taking a deep breath, she switched the flashlight on. With the flashlight, she could see that the stairs continued to descend into the old catacombs below Rome.

"Are you sure this is where the priest said to go?" Dash asked, his voice full of doubt. They had managed to find a priest that had spoken to Alec recently. The man had sent them into the catacombs, where he'd told Alec to go in search of the Book of Anu.

"Nicole ... are you even listening to me?" Dash asked again.

"Yes," Nicole answered in a low voice, as she tried to keep from breathing in too deeply and gagging. The stench of decay that mingled with the musty air in the tunnels was nauseating. Nicole found that it took extensive concentration to keep from vomiting. Suddenly she felt as if the room was spinning and she reached out to steady herself with the wall, but then she remembered the corpses that lined the tunnels of the catacombs.

"Do you need me to hold you up?" Dash asked, amused at her human frailty.

"No ... I'm fine," she told him, though she was anything but fine. Someone was watching them - she could feel their eyes drilling into her head. The evil that radiated from those unseen eyes was so strong that a chill made its way up her spine.

It was waiting for them!

The thought jumped out at her as if someone were screaming it in her ear. In that moment she was tempted to turn back. But if Alec were in the catacombs, he was in as much danger as they were. Taking a deep breath, Nicole moved forward. She'd just find Alec and then they'd get out.

If she could find Alec! The dark voice of doubt forced its way into her head.

"Stop," Dash hissed.

Nicole froze.

"There's something up ahead," he whispered.

"I know. I've been feeling it for a few minutes now."

"Let me go ahead," Dash said, stepping in front of her.

Nicole moved aside so that he could get ahead of her.

Dash came to a sudden stop. "Turn off the light."

Nicole did as he asked. "What is it?"

Dash motioned for her to be quiet, but after a few moments he started moving again. "I still think there's something down here," he told her in a low voice.

Nicole didn't respond. She continued to listen intently for any sounds that seemed out of place, but all she could hear were their footsteps echoing through the tunnels. She felt a chill on her arm. That's the first thing that her mind registered - the touch was so cold. Then she felt pain as the hand clamped down on her arm and pulled her into the darkness.

Nicole screamed, and Dash caught sight of her just as she was being pulled into a passageway. She was being dragged across the rough ground. The rock and dirt dug at her bare flesh, but she did not feel the sting of her wounds, only the terror of the unknown.

Dash was following as quickly as he could, but the creature that had a hold of her was faster.

Though she struggled to pull her arm away from her captor, she knew if she pulled anymore, her limb would come right out of its socket. Again she screamed, hoping someone - anyone would hear her.

* * * *

Sarah was unaccustomed to so many people crammed into one place. Though she'd gone out with friends while at school in Portland, she'd not done so frequently. The Tiger's Lair was one of the most popular clubs with the students in Reno, at least that was what Summer had told her. With the crowd dancing almost shoulder to shoulder, Sarah thought for sure every student in Reno must be at the club.

Summer had already introduced her to several of her friends, but a moment after she walked away, Sarah couldn't even recall their names. Her mind was hundreds of miles away, in Sutter Point. The flashing lights of the nightclub couldn't hold her interest like the memory of Darrien's lovemaking. Even as she tried to force the memory away so that she could at least try and enjoy her night out, she kept seeing his face, and how his passion could set fire to his cold - mesmerizing eyes.

Sarah kept to the dark corners of the club. From where she was sitting, she could see Summer with a group of people. The men seemed to flock around her, but Summer appeared to be completely unaware of the power she wielded over the opposite sex.

Sipping at her drink, Sarah was content to watch Summer have all the fun. Her friend tried to get her to come with her while she mingled with the crowd, but Sarah just didn't feel comfortable. She much preferred the dark corner.

"Would you like to dance?"

Sarah's attention was drawn to the man that stood at the side of her table, a smile pasted across his face. He was the exact opposite of Darrien. He had a deeply tanned complexion and sun bleached blond hair. His blue eyes seemed to dance with mischief. Sarah found this a refreshing change from Darrien's dismal moods.

Sarah hesitated only a moment before nodding and setting her drink on the table. The man held out his hand to her and she took it. His hand was warm, so much different than Darrien's cold touch.

Why did she keep comparing this stranger to Darrien?

He led her through the crowd to the dance floor and then pulled her into his arms. "What's your name?" he asked.

"Sarah," she said, forcing a smile. It wasn't that she didn't want to be dancing with such a handsome man, she just wished she could stop thinking of Darrien.

"Well Sarah, I'm Anthony," he told her as he was leading her into a slow dance.

A moment into the dance, Sarah felt eyes on her. It was that tingling sensation that you get when you know someone is watching you. Sarah's eyes scanned the room, searching the faces of the crowd to see who it was that had their attention on her.

Finally she spotted him. He stood in the shadows - away from the crowd. His eyes were like blades, and at that very moment, they were slicing her to shreds. She could feel his anger, even from across the club with a swarm of people between them.

Sarah caught her breath. His was the last face that she'd expected to see in the crowd, but there he was. Darrien had found her.

Had it been her spell, or would he have found her anyway?

Sarah now wished that she hadn't cast her spell the night before. Darrien was moving toward her, but she pretended not to notice as she snuggled closer to the guy she was dancing with. A little jealousy wouldn't hurt him, particularly after he'd called her by another woman's name.

Then he was standing next to them, glaring at her dancing companion. "Do you mind if I finish this dance?" he asked Anthony. Though it was a request, it was clear that he would take the man's place, even if he did have any objections.

Anthony nodded his head and turned to Sarah. "It was nice meeting you. I hope I get the opportunity to see you again."

Sarah smiled at him. "Yes, it was nice meeting you too."

Anthony disappeared into the crowd and Darrien wrapped his arms around her waist. "What are you doing?" he asked, his words alive with fury.

"I was dancing," she answered, forcing a light tone to her voice.

"You are out here where anyone can see you, when you know that you are being hunted."

"No one knows where I am. At least no one knew until you found me," Sarah told him, her mouth turned down in a frown.

"If I can find you, so can they." Darrien glared at her.

"How *did* you find me?" she asked, but without meeting his eyes. She knew it had been her spell that had led Darrien to Reno.

"The lycan that brought you here felt compelled to divulge your location to your father. Donavan Ashe sent me here to take you back to New Orleans. He feels that you would be safer under his care."

"If he was so worried about my safety, where has he been all these years? Why didn't he come to get me himself?" Sarah's bitterness was evident.

"I asked if I could come for you," Darrien told her. "As for the rest of it … you'll have to bring up your questions to your father."

"Well I think I'm just fine where I'm at," she told him, lifting her chin defiantly.

"Regardless of what you think, you will be coming with me."

"And if I don't?" Sarah asked, knowing what his answer would be.

"Then I will take you against your will," he growled. To prove his point, he started pulling her toward the exit.

"Wait! I have to tell my friend that I'm leaving," Sarah insisted.

Darrien shook his head. "I have already taken the liberty of collecting your things from her apartment and leaving a note for you."

Sarah glared at him. "She will think that something happened to me."

"No … she doesn't realize that you are being hunted by vampires. Lex only told her that you were having some family problems. That is … unless you've told her otherwise, and I don't believe you have." Darrien was smiling.

Sarah found his arrogance infuriating. "Why don't you go chase Caroline's ghost and leave me be?"

"I am ... chasing Caroline's ghost that is." Darrien's eyes turned cold. "Now why don't we enjoy our dance?" he said, pulling her closer so that his lips were right next to her ear.

Darrien gently caressed her back while his lips went to her neck. He was kissing her and biting at her flesh. Sarah began to shake, her need for him overcoming caution.

"Want to go somewhere?" he asked, even as he was skillfully moving her toward the exit of the Tiger's Lair.

"Does my father know what we have been doing when we're alone?" Sarah questioned him, but she didn't resist when he pulled her out the door and into the night.

Darrien's dark laughter unnerved her. "If he did ... I probably wouldn't be here right now."

Before Sarah could respond, she found herself in his arms and rising above the nightclub. The view of Reno was breathtaking from such heights, but she saw none of it. Darrien's kiss drew her in, refusing to let her experience anything but his desire - his utter and complete need of her.

Sarah was barely aware when they landed on the top of a tall building. Darrien drew her into the darkness so that they would be hidden from the lights of the city. His teeth were on her skin, piercing at her flesh, as he violently tore away the silk dress she was wearing. Cupping her bare breasts in his hands, he fell to his knees and took one hard nipple into his mouth.

The searing need between her legs erupted into an inferno of pure lust when she felt his fangs scraping against her tender flesh. Her hands strayed to his hair. She delighted in the feel of his silky mane as she ran her fingers through it, pulling him even closer.

"I'm not Caroline," she breathed. She wanted him so fiercely that she was like a woman possessed, but she needed to hear her name on his lips when he took her.

"I don't care! I must have you now." Darrien's voice trembled with his barely controlled lust - his need to possess her.

Darrien pulled her to her knees and his mouth took hers. He kissed her deeply, sucking and biting at her tongue until she was squirming just to keep from demanding that he fulfill her need with this flesh.

Sarah peeled away his black leather jacket so that she could feel his cool skin and his muscles rippling beneath her hands. Darrien moved until he was positioned behind her. She heard the sharp sound of him lowering the zipper on his pants. She then felt his stiff flesh resting against the back of her thighs.

The sound of her panties being ripped from her body cut through the stillness that surrounded them. Sarah gasped, anticipating the moment that he would fill her with his need, and bring her the released that she craved. She felt him slide between her legs, teasing her moist heat with the promise of fulfilling her utterly. It was the promise of absolute ecstasy when he finally took her.

"Say my name," she gasped.

"Hmm … Sarah … I want you Sarah," Darrien's smooth voice was like an aphrodisiac that sent her over the edge of reason.

Wiggling her hips against him, she tried to force him inside of her, but he continued to tease, letting her feel only the silky head of his erection.

"Once we do this … there's no taking it back," he warned, though he continued to tease her until she was sure she would explode from within.

"I want it." Sarah's voice cracked. The effort to speak was too much to deal with while her body burned for him with such intensity.

Darrien mounted her before the last word left her mouth, and a small scream escaped her lips as he parted her flesh with his throbbing tool.

At last he was within her and she could finally feel him as intimately as was possible for two separate beings to feel each other. The sensation was akin to being reborn as one.

As he moved within her, he pulled her with him to unimagined heights of pleasure - pleasure that was like nothing that she had ever experienced. Sarah pushed against him hard, trying to feel even more of him. Darrien made love to her with the skill that only an immortal could possess - giving her pain and pleasure within the same instant.

With his hands on her hips, he held her tight against him. Leaning over her, he sank his teeth into her back. Tenderly, he slid his tongue across her skin, licking up the droplets of blood that dripped from her wounds.

Just when she was sure that the fire would sear her flesh, she felt him pulsate within her as he spilled his seed into her body. She started shaking with the force of the pleasure that ripped through her, beginning at the core of her womanhood and spreading to every nerve ending in her body.

Sarah's screams of ecstasy were quickly cut off when he clamped a hand over her mouth.

"Shhh ... you'll attract attention," he whispered.

When Darrien moved away from her, Sarah sat up and stared down at her tattered dress. Darrien had shredded the silky material and now it no longer covered her sufficiently. Sensing her dilemma, Darrien draped his leather jacket over her shoulders.

"Thank you," she told him, an uncertain smile tugging at her lips. Their lovemaking had been nothing short of unbelievable. But Sarah could not help but wonder if it was she he had made love to, or Caroline.

Darrien gave her a feather soft kiss on the lips. "What's troubling you," he asked. "Do you regret what happened?"

Sarah shook her head. "No ... I could never regret what we've had.

From the top of the building the view of the city was captivating. The neon lights of the casinos lit up the streets below, but on the rooftop the darkness shielded them - wrapping them in a blanket of enchantment that could not be penetrated by the outside world - at least not yet.

Darrien pulled her into his arms. "So tell me what's wrong?"

"I'm Sarah ... not Caroline."

"It doesn't matter," he whispered and kissed her again. "I love you no matter who you are."

"What will happen with us? I mean when this is all over?" Sarah looked over at him, wanting to hear that he would be with her always, but somehow knowing that wasn't what he would say.

Darrien seemed completely engrossed in the city lights. When he spoke he refused to look at her. "You and I, we are very different Sarah. If I am unlucky ... I will live forever, but death will claim you at some point, even if it's when you are old and have lived a full life. I cannot watch you die ... not again."

"There you go again, thinking I am Caroline." Sarah pulled away from him.

"When is my birthday Sarah?" he asked, his question seemingly off topic.

"June 10, 1735," Sarah answered quickly - too quickly.

Darrien lifted his hands. "Now how would you have known that ... if you are not Caroline? I have never told you what my birthday is, at least not while you were Sarah."

"Maybe I am reading you? I can do that sometimes."

"Yes, I'm sure you can, but you can't read me Sarah. I'm a vampire, and that would be difficult ... even for a psychic. Only the oldest and most powerful vampires can read other vampires."

"Okay then, I'm picking up Caroline's spirit ... her memories," Sarah shrugged.

"Close your eyes Sarah. Remember the first time we spoke. Go back to that time and relive it as if you were there."

Sarah closed her eyes and instead of darkness, she saw a field of wildflowers. Darrien was there, at the gates of the chateau. He was riding a black horse. Unlike the many times that she'd seen him out riding, on that day he noticed her right away, and waved. Through the years she'd watched him from a distance, but that day had been the first time he'd acknowledged her.

When she waved back, he started riding toward her. Looking down, she could see that she was no longer Sarah, but Caroline. She wore the woman's brown cotton skirt and leather shoes. Although she felt extremely unattractive in such unflattering garments, she need not have worried. To Darrien she'd been the vision of perfection with her long auburn hair resembling a cascade of fire, and green eyes that sparkled like jewels. He had been unable to take his eyes from her.

Darrien pulled up on the horse's reins and stared at her as if he'd never seen her before.

Caroline fixed her eyes on the wildflowers she held in her hand. "My lord."

"Are you not Caroline Fabre?" he asked.

"Yes my lord."

"Call me Darrien," he told her.

Caroline didn't respond. She continued to stare at the flowers, afraid of what her eyes would reveal if she looked on his face. Too many times she had dreamt of this moment - longed to hear him say her name, and now he was here and talking to her.

"Do you know how to ride?" he asked.

Caroline shook her head, not trusting herself to speak. She was filled with too much anxiety.

Darrien held out his hand to her. "Come ... we will ride together. I would like to know more about Caroline Fabre."

She'd gone with him that day and everyday after, for weeks. They'd make love in a grove of trees, far from prying eyes. Though she'd known that she would never be more than a diversion to him, she could not help but hope that just maybe it might be different with her than it had been with the others. She'd heard the rumors about Darrien and the servant girls. How he'd take them for his pleasure and disregard them when done. Each day she vowed to love him forever - if he would only do the same.

Then the day came that he did not show up for their ride. He didn't come the next day, or the next. She'd been heartbroken, but as the months passed, she moved beyond her pain and eventually married.

When Sarah opened her eyes she was yanked back to the present. This time she was as one with Caroline. She experienced the same love for him, and the same pain.

"How dare you treat me like that?" she seethed.

"Now you remember?" he smiled.

"You left me without a word!"

"I had no choice," he defended himself. "Omar attacked me with the intention of turning me and gaining control over my father's domain in France. As soon as my father found out, he sent me away, despite the fact that he should have destroyed me instead. I had to go away and could not return to you the next day, or any day."

"But you could have come to me in the night," she insisted.

"Yes I could have, but what could I have offered you?" The hard glint in his eyes had disappeared to be replaced by sorrow.

"You could have at least told me, instead of letting me believe that you'd disregarded me like trash." Sarah felt a lump forming in her throat. Though she had not lived through the pain and the memories that she was experiencing, they were real to her.

"Try to remember … I did come back to you eventually," he told her softly.

Visions of darkness and the horror of what he'd become filled her mind. The memories came back like a relentless storm, pounding at her heart until she was in tears.

There was that dark spirit - the one that had threatened to take the life of her child if she accepted his kiss of immortality.

"You were the last person I saw before I died," she told him, her voice soft and full of sorrow.

"I know. I wanted it to be that way. I wanted you to go from life seeing the face of someone that loved you." Darrien kissed her again, this time putting so much emotion in it that she could feel it radiating from his soul.

"My baby?" Sarah asked, pulling away from him.

Darrien put a finger up to her lips. "Shhh … she was taken to safety. Otherwise the Fabre witches would not be … would they?"

"But what about us? Promise me that you will not go away again."

At her words, Darrien again turned away. "I cannot give you that promise. As I said, I will not bring death to you again."

"That is what you do when you turn away from me," Sarah told him, hoping that he would see reason.

"Let's not waste time," he told her. "We have right now and that's what is important."

His mouth covered hers when she tried to protest. Though she let herself get lost in his kiss, she vowed that this time they would not be parted.

Chapter Sixteen

Deep within the catacombs below Rome, is a place of darkness - a place so black that the darkness itself seems to be alive. That darkness wrapped itself around Nicole - mocking the human weakness that prevented her from seeing what was hidden within the black void of the tomb. Her arm throbbed, but the pain only scratched the surface of her consciousness. Even the intense throbbing of her dislocated shoulder could not overcome the terror that crawled through her mind – taking control of her thoughts.

The last thing she remembered was someone or something dragging her through the tunnels by her arm, and then the excruciating pain that had sent her into nothingness. When Nicole opened her eyes - nothing changed. If anything, it seemed even darker than when her eyes were closed. She felt around the wall near her and concluded that she was in some type of small room - closed in by a heavy wooden door. She tried to pull the door open with her good arm, but it wouldn't budge.

Dash had been right behind her, chasing her abductor, but as far as she could tell he wasn't in the room with her.

What had happened to Dash?

Fear chewed at her insides. Had he simply lost her in the chase, or had something happened to him?

Nicole's breath caught in her throat at the sound of rattling chains somewhere in the darkness, not far from where she lay on the cold earthen floor. Memories of what Omar had done to Ethan pounded through her head.

"Dash!" she called out, her voice seemed small in the thick - inky void.

She heard a growl and then the sound of rattling chains grew louder. Whoever was bound in those chains was trying to break free.

"Dash! Is that you?"

Again there was no answer but a series of angry growls, and then silence. A moment later the silence was shattered by the harsh sound of a lock releasing. The door swung open and the bright light of a torch blinded Nicole. She could not see who carried the torch, but she guessed it to be whoever had dragged her into the hole where she was being held prisoner.

As her eyes adjusted to the light, Nicole saw the shape of a woman behind the light.

"Isn't this cozy?" the female voice was poisonous.

As Julia's face came into focus, Nicole's despair grew. Next to the female vampire was a man that she assumed was also a vampire. Her companion's eyes radiated hunger, his short-cropped white hair and his pasty complexion made him appear more specter than vampire.

Julia was the definition of pure evil. It had been Julia that had been so instrumental when Omar had taken Nicole captive with the intention of turning her. It had also been Julia that had turned Alec so long ago. Julia was angry, and she directed that anger at Nicole. Alec had made it clear to Julia that he would not treat her as his mistress, and that he preferred Nicole to her.

Now Julia directed her fury at both of them.

Nicole blinked, trying to force her gaze away from the vampire's cold eyes.

"So Donavan's human brat is awake?" she glowered at Nicole.

Nicole said nothing.

"Good ... I want you awake when I let your vampire lover loose on you," Julia told her, nodding toward the darkness behind Nicole.

Nicole looked to her side and saw who had been rattling chains. Visions of Ethan's deformed features mingled with the horror of what she was seeing at that moment. Blood deprivation - it would turn a vampire into a true monster. Alec did not seem to be quite as far gone as Ethan had been, when Omar had deprived him of feeding for weeks, but he was not the Alec that she knew.

His blue eyes were alight with bloodlust, and a hunger she'd never seen in them before. When he drew back his cracked lips, his fangs protruded abnormally, as if he were drying up - becoming a shell. The growls that ripped from his throat were that of a creature that had no thought but to go with the hunger that controlled him.

"Why are you doing this to him?" Nicole cried. "It is me that Omar wants."

"As noble as your thoughts are … doing it this way is just easier. We get rid of you both, and I get to watch the horror on Alec's face when he comes to his senses and realizes that he fed on his beloved human bitch." Julia's face twisted with hate.

Julia turned to her companion. "Let him go and we'll leave her to him," she told the male vampire before placing the torch in a bracket attached to the wall.

"Nooo!" Alec's growled, as he yanked at the chains that bound his arms.

Julia laughed. "Will you be able to resist your hunger Alec? Will you die in agony so that she will live? Somehow I doubt it."

When Alec was free, the two vampires left the room, locking the door behind them.

Instead of lunging toward Nicole, Alec fell to the ground and rolled into a ball. With howls of agony, he began tearing at his hair. The aching in Nicole's heart subdued her fear. His pain was her pain, and she could not endure it. Getting to her hands and knees, she crawled to where he lay.

"Go away," he snarled, trying to roll away from her.

Nicole unbuttoned her blouse so that her breasts were bare. It would be safer than him feeding from the artery in her neck. "Feed from me," she urged in a low voice.

Alec ignored her and continued to wither in pain on the cold floor.

Nicole leaned closer to him until her breast brushed against his face. "Please … take what you need," she told him.

Nicole gasped at the sudden sensation of pain when his fangs sank into her tender flesh. He was ravenous, and as he fed, she could feel her strength ebbing and the warmth leaving her body.

* * * *

Sarah sat at the cave's entrance, watching as the sun descended into the western horizon. Behind her, the darkness of the cave provided a safe haven for Darrien as he slept. That was how they traveled. By day they would find shelter from the sun, most often a cave, but an abandoned building would do as well, if it had a basement. At night they would travel.

Darrien had found a motorbike at a truck stop. Taking it by force from the owner. The biker had resisted, until he'd seen Darrien's ugly side. After that, the man had been more than happy to let them take his bike, as long as they left him alone.

Before sunrise Darrien would find shelter. When he thought Sarah was asleep, he left her so that he could hunt. Sarah let him believe that she didn't know what he did when he was gone, but she knew. She watched him leave and return with the hunger gone from his eyes.

After three nights of travel they entered the Ozarks. There were caves to hide in, but after tonight there would be no more caves to offer shelter. When they entered Louisiana, there would be swamp. Darrien had informed her that once they were in Louisiana they might be forced to turn to the above ground tombs for shelter. Unless they could make it all the way to New Orleans, but that was doubtful. The thought of sleeping in a tomb sent shivers down her spine. What stories would the dead tell her? What horror and heartbreak would she live through their memories and pain?

As the light faded, she heard Darrien stirring from within the shadows of the cave. From behind, she felt him wrap his arms around her.

"Did you get any sleep?" he asked.

"A little."

Darrien gently moved her long hair out of the way so that he could kiss the back of her neck. "I want you again," he whispered.

His touch and the desire in his voice sent shivers through her body. They had made love before she'd gone to sleep, and everyday since leaving Reno. Still her need for him was as great as it had been the first time they'd come together.

Being the object of his desire was pure heaven, but Sarah could not shake the feeling that he wanted to make love to her so much, because he knew there would be no tomorrow, at least not for them. Sarah would not voice her doubts - she would not taint their time together with regret.

Sarah leaned her head back to look at him, and she felt his lips on hers. His kiss was tender, but with an underlying heat that could not be denied. When the kiss ended, Sarah smiled at him.

"I'm starving. We can't live on love alone," she told him.

"I know … unfortunately," he scowled. "What do you want to eat?"

"A cheeseburger," she told him mischievously. She knew that he would have much preferred to go in search of a rabbit, and cook it over a fire for her.

"A cheeseburger?" Darrien drew his brows together. "And which hamburger stand did you want my dear? The one at mile marker 128 … or the joint near mile marker 150?"

Sarah stuck her tongue out at him and giggled. "I can wait until the next town."

A wicked gleam entered his eyes and he started moving toward her. "I don't know if I can wait that long to eat."

Sarah laughed and backed away from him, but Darrien quickly tackled her to the ground. "You would be a nice little scrap to tide me over," he whispered.

Sarah placed her hands on both sides of his face, and peered into his dark eyes. "I love you."

The laughter fled from his eyes. "I know you do," he told her, and then his lips devoured hers as he kissed her hungrily.

Sarah pulled away so that she could catch her breath. "Darrien ... I don't want to live without you." The tightness in her throat made it nearly impossible to say the words.

Darrien rolled off of her and sat up. "Sarah, please don't ask me to do it again. I love you too much to see you die, or to witness the ravages of time take you from me."

"But what about what I feel? Doesn't that matter?" Sarah shot back angrily.

"Yes, of course it does."

"Then stay with me Darrien. There has to be a way for you to turn me. Maybe that would make you feel better about it, but do not make me endure life without you," Sarah pleaded.

"We should be going," Darrien told her as he stood up.

Sarah frowned. With a sigh, she began gathering the few belongings that she'd been able to bring with her.

Every time she brought up the subject, Darrien would clam up on her and become distant. Sarah was finally beginning to see how her mother could have been so possessed with her need, that she would risk anything to be with the man she loved.

Suddenly a thought occurred to her. "I know that you mentioned my father, but you didn't say anything about my mother. Is she with him?"

"I don't know anything about her," Darrien told her, but he would not meet her eyes.

"Darrien I can feel it ... you are lying. What do you know about my mother?"

"That is something that you need to bring up with your father. It isn't my place."

Without saying anymore, Sarah continued to watch him. He was hiding something from her, and from the look on his face she suspected that whatever he was keeping from her, was not pleasant.

* * * *

The rope around his neck made it impossible to move without cutting off the blood flow to his brain. According to myth, the vampire does not live, so there is no blood flow. If only that were true he would really be invulnerable. Unfortunately for Dash, the slayers knew which myths were true and which were simply stories told over hundreds of years - years in which the human population had grown to hate and fear the creatures of the night.

In the flickering candlelight, the chapel above the catacombs of St. Domitilla seemed far more sinister than holy.

"You must listen to me," Dash's voice was weak as the slayer pulled the noose tighter.

The end of the rope was draped over the rafters above the altar. When they tired of torturing him, they could simply pull on the rope and hang him until he lost consciousness. They would then decapitate him and burn his remains. This way they could be sure that he would not reanimate.

When Dash had emerged from the catacombs below, and entered the chapel in search of help for Nicole, the two men came out of nowhere. They were slayers, the worst kind of killers. They killed mercilessly if you were a vampire.

With the two slayers was a priest, and though he was an older man, he was no less formidable. It was the priest that had recognized him for a vampire, when Nicole approached the man to ask him about Alec. Though Dash had hung back, what he was had been obvious to the priest. But Dash hadn't guessed that the man was also a slayer.

"My friend is in trouble down there." His words were cut off as one of the slayers pulled the rope tight.

The priest's hard eyes rested on Dash's face. "Why would we care what happens to a vampire? You are the spawn of Satan, and we must send you back to the hell from which you came."

"I know of no Satan," Dash strained against the unyielding noose, forcing the words from his mouth. "And hell … hell is the curse of eternal darkness."

"Repent now! Beg God to have mercy on your soul!" the priest roared.

A laugh escaped his dry and injured throat. "Sorry … I did that a long time ago."

An instant after the last word left his mouth, a spray of holy water hit him in the face, but his flesh did not blister and burn.

"Please! Destroy me if you must, but help my friend. She is no vampire and her life is in danger."

Father Rovati motioned with his hand for the slayers to loosen the noose's hold on Dash's neck.

"Is this some trick?" he asked Dash.

"She's in the catacombs. We were ambushed by these … these things. I hesitate to call them vampires," he added.

"What kind of rubbish is this?" The priest's anger surfaced.

"She is searching for the one that talked with you about the Book of Anu."

The priest seemed to withdraw, silently contemplating Dash's words.

"How many?" Father Rovati finally asked.

"Two that I know of. They drug her away and I could not keep up. When I searched for her, she was gone. I think they have her hidden," Dash explained, his face twisting into a painful grimace. The effort to speak was almost too much - the pain too great.

"Why would you care what happens to her?" Rovati narrowed his eyes, suspicious of Dash's words.

"She's my friend," Dash told him.

The priest's eyes rested on the two slayers that had accompanied him into the chapel. "Let him go. He can lead us to these other vampires, and the girl."

Chapter Seventeen

Alec shook uncontrollably - the grief and the self-loathing too much to endure. Tears spilled from his eyes as he stared down at the unmoving form in his arms. She was so pale - so lifeless. He knew it would only be a matter of moments before she succumbed to the ultimate sleep. Death would claim her, and it was he that had brought it to her.

This is what Julia wanted. She wanted him to feel this self-hate and disdain for what he was. She was amused by the fact that it would ultimately be his hunger that would steal the last breath of his humanity.

A small amount of blood still oozed from the wound on her breast, it lay scarlet against her pale skin. The sight did not invoke his hunger, only the pain of knowing that he had killed the only person that mattered to him. He had doused the single flicker of light that had still illuminated his world of darkness.

His hunger had been too great. He had tried to withdraw from her, but his need to feed had consumed him. When he'd finally come to his senses, Nicole had grown limp and pale - her life essence nearly gone. She'd sacrificed herself to ease his suffering, but the pain of taking her life was far greater than the agony of starvation could ever be.

Alec closed his eyes so that he would not need to see her face as she died. But even then he could still see her beautiful - pale face in his mind's eye. Nothing would take away this moment. He did not even have the blissful nothingness of death to look forward to.

Nicole's breath rattled deep within her chest, and with one last gasp it, was gone.

Alec cradled Nicole's body while she suffered through the throes of death. The only way he could have saved her was to turn her, but he knew that is not what she would want. How could he condemn her to the same hell that he wished to end for himself?

* * * *

Nicole looked down on the scene below. She saw her own body and Alec's unbearable grief. She could feel his pain and wanted to comfort him, but he was oblivious to her presence.

She knew her body had died, but somehow that didn't matter. All that mattered to her was the pain that her death was causing to the man that was her heart - the one being that had mattered to her more than life itself.

Nicole drifted down from the ceiling and reached out to touch him, but her hand went through his arm. She was nothing more than energy now. He would never hear her words again, nor feel her touch.

"Nicki." The small voice seemed to come from everywhere at the same time. It surrounded her with warmth.

There was a golden light - a light so bright that it should have blinded her, but she no longer had her mortal eyes. She looked upon the light with the eyes of the dead. Silhouetted in that light, was the form of a small boy. Nicole knew it was her little brother, Jay. She could feel the love within him radiate toward her - showering her soul with a love so complete that it could not be experienced in life.

"Jay," Nicole called to him - not with her mortal voice, but with her mind.

Then he was there - standing right in front of her. As he held out his small hand to her, it occurred to Nicole that he appeared as beautiful and healthy as he had in life, maybe even more so.

"Nicki … you should not be here." His small voice was just as she remembered it, but so crystal clear, and loving that she knew it was truly the voice of an angel.

"I've missed you so much." Nicole's words were pure thought, but she could still hear them in her head as if she were speaking them.

Jay shook his head. "Come with me."

The instant Nicole took his hand she was gone from the tomb where her life had ended, but the part of her soul that could not let go of Alec, yearned to stay behind.

"Come Nicki ... come and see." Jay's voice was a melody of heaven. For so long his voice had been inaudible to her in life, and she could not help but submerge herself in it now.

Then she was somewhere else. It was dark, but flickering candlelight cut through that darkness. On the stone floor, a young girl lay curled up in a ball, sleeping. Right now the girl was alone, but Nicole sensed that someone had been there. The darkness of the immortal still hung in the air like a black fog that no light could penetrate.

"Your sister," Jay told her.

"Why do you show me this now?"

As soon as the thought formed, he was answering her.

"Her name is Sarah. She can hear you ... she can help you."

"Sarah,"

As quickly as the name entered Nicole's thoughts, the girl blinked rapidly and opened her eyes.

* * * *

Dash walked ahead of the slayers, a rope wrapped around his upper body to keep him from trying to escape. Every few moments one of them would prod him with a wooden staff that they each carried with them.

Never before had he come this close to a slayer. Father Rovati was in the lead, carrying a torch to help light the way. If the vampires were still in the catacombs, the priest would see them first, but he seemed to have no fear of the immortals.

"Hey father, do you think it such a good idea to go ahead of us?" Dash asked.

"They can take my life but not my soul. That is all that I need worry about."

Dash wished that he had the confidence of the priest, but he knew better. The vampires could take your body and soul - at least to the point that heaven no longer mattered - if it existed at all.

"How much further?" Rovati asked him.

Up ahead of them, Dash saw that the tunnel curved to the right. "It was just after that turn that they grabbed her. They drug her for a bit before I lost them." Just as he spoke the last word, Dash felt the air stir in front of him, and he heard Father Rovati cry out.

There was a blur of movement and he saw the priest pull a machete from his robes. With liquid-smooth movement, the blade cut through the vampire's neck, and his head rolled to the ground.

Just beyond the light of the torch, there was more movement and the two slayers moved past Dash to run into the darkness. The sounds of struggle echoed through the tunnels, and Dash felt the dread of someone that would soon be facing his executioner. If the slayers failed, he would be killed as a traitor.

To lead a slayer to another vampire was an unforgivable sin among the immortals. He'd only done it to save Nicole, but that wouldn't matter in the end. None of it really mattered. Even if the slayers did kill the vampires, the humans would destroy him. The only real difference being that if he were killed by the slayers, death would be quick - not so with the immortals.

The howling scream of a vampire could be heard over the commotion ahead of them. There was another scream. This scream was different - it was a scream of pure anguish, and with that scream the howling of a single word - a name.

Nicole.

* * * *

Sarah stared at the vapor-like image that peered at her from a dark corner of the tomb. The woman's black hair was in contrast to her extremely pale face. The white-translucent color of her skin was unusual, even for a ghost. The dark eyes that stared back at Sarah were like orbs of night. But unlike the emptiness or anger that Sarah usually encountered with earth bound spirits, the woman's eyes were curious. There was something else in the girl's eyes that Sarah found unsettling - fear.

Sarah pushed herself into a sitting position, thinking that as soon as she moved the specter would disappear, but it didn't.

"Sarah." The woman's voice seemed to come from far away, as if she were on a phone call with a bad connection.

"Who are you and what do you want?" Sarah asked.

Though she had been dealing with spirits her entire life, it always startled her when one showed up next to her while she was sleeping.

"I am Nicole ... your sister."

Lex's words suddenly came back to her. She had sisters - two of them. They had to fight some conspiracy her uncle was perpetrating.

How could they do that if one of them was dead?

"This is important," the woman told her. "You must do something for me ... and do it quickly."

"What?" Sarah asked, worried about what she would be asked to do. Most often the dead wanted her to make contact with the living, but Sarah knew she was in no position to do so right now. Not with Omar's vamps hunting her.

"Call my phone." Nicole's voice was hollow, but still the urgency of the request was clear. "Give a message to the person that answers the phone."

Sarah's thoughts went to the phone in her purse. Darrien had asked her to turn it off. He worried that they would be tracked through the GPS system built into her mobile. If they had found a way to track her through her mobile, it could be very risky to turn it on.

"Please!" The ghostly voice begged. "You are the only person that can help me."

Sarah shrugged and reached for her purse. Somehow she doubted that Omar had turned to technology to find her. From everything she had heard, this vampire seemed to be someone stuck in the past - refusing to accept anything that is new or different.

Pulling the phone from her purse, she held down the on button. A moment later the screen came to life, but there was no reception.

"I'm not getting any service," she told her sister's ghost.

"Go outside."

Sarah got to her feet and walked quickly to the entrance of the tomb. Pushing the door open, she stepped out into the night. All around her were monuments to the dead, stark white tombs against a black sky.

From the corner of her eye she saw the movement of shadow. She jumped and was ready to flee when Darrien stepped out from behind a nearby crypt.

"What are you doing?" he asked.

"Making a phone call," she told him as she looked around for the ghost that had urged her to go outside.

"I'm still here," Nicole whispered in her ear. Sarah could hear her, but now she couldn't see her.

"Now what?" Sarah asked.

"What do you mean?" Darrien stepped closer, but Sarah held up her hand to stop him.

"I'm not talking to you," she told him.

"What do you mean you're not talking to me? Who are you talking to then?"

Sarah wasn't listening to him. She quickly dialed the number Nicole was giving her.

The phone rang on the other end, but no one was picking it up.

* * * *

At the sound of Nicole's name, Dash sprinted forward, barely noticing when he was forced to step over Julia's decapitated body. Now he stood behind the priest while the man broke through the locked door. Beyond the door, they could still hear the cries of agony that had led them to the hidden tomb. As they stepped inside, Dash felt his stomach twist into knots at the spectacle that greeted them.

Alec still cradled Nicole's body in his arms, his features marred by the pain and torment that ripped at his soul.

"You fed on her!" Dash yelled as he flew toward Alec in full attack mode. But he was still bound with rope, and the priest's slayers managed to take him to the ground.

Alec's voice shook with a depth of emotion rarely shown by an immortal. "I beg of you ... destroy me, but please take her back to New Orleans. She must be laid to rest with her little brother. She should be near those that loved her in life."

"You bloodsucker!" Again Dash tried to break away so that he could get at Alec.

Father Rovati turned to glare at Dash. "Be still!"

Kneeling beside Nicole, the priest placed a finger at her neck to check for a pulse. "We are too late ... she is gone," he announced.

Dash wailed, overcome by the agony of loss.

"You did this?" Father Rovati's hard eyes fell on Alec.

"They kept me from feeding, and locked her in with me. I tried to resist, but ... she would not let me suffer."

An eerie silence descended on them as all eyes rested on Nicole's pale form. The stillness of the moment was shattered when the mobile phone in Nicole's pocket began to ring.

Chapter Eighteen

The sound of the phone seemed to spur the priest into action and he turned to the two slayers. "In the chapel is my emergency bag. Get it quickly!"

Both of the men took off and Father Rovati turned to Alec. "There is a chance we can save her."

Alec shook his head. "She is already gone."

"We have a small window, but I must act now," Rovati began performing CPR on her.

"It is important that we get what blood she has left, circulating." Father Rovati told them as he was pushing down on Nicole's chest in an effort to get her heart to work.

The phone kept ringing, but it was ignored. Dash and Alec were engrossed in watching the priest. A moment later, the two men returned with a large black bag.

The phone had become silent.

"Take over!" the priest told Alec.

Alec did as he was told without a second thought. He did not believe it would help, but he was ready to grasp at any chance of saving her, no matter how small that chance was.

Father Rovati pulled a small cooler from the bag and opened it quickly. Inside were several IV bags of blood. He hooked the bags to an IV tube with a flow chamber and a needle. The priest then inserted the needle and started the blood flowing while Alec continued to perform chest compressions.

"What if it is the wrong blood type?" Dash asked.

"It's O Rh negative. It won't hurt her ... anymore than she already is in any case." Rovati told him while motioning for Alec to stop.

The priest quickly checked for a pulse, before continuing the chest compressions himself.

Again the phone began to ring.

"Will someone get that?" Rovati panted, obviously the effort to resurrect Nicole taking its toll on the old priest.

Alec pulled the phone out of Nicole's pants pocket. "Hello."

A female voice came on the line. "I have a message from Nicole."

Alec frowned. "Who is this? What kind of joke are you trying to pull?"

"No ... wait! Don't hang up," she said just as Alec was ready to end the call. "She said to tell you that your blood can reanimate her, without turning her."

Alec was silent.

"Do it now!" the girl yelled.

Alec dropped the phone. "Give her my blood," he told the priest.

Rovati looked at him. "I cannot be responsible for turning her."

"She won't turn. Please ... just try it."

In a flurry of movement, the priest quickly inserted the transfusion line into one of Alec's veins, so that Nicole would begin getting his blood.

Within seconds Nicole was gasping for air, and the color slowly started coming back to her face. When Nicole's breathing was steady, Rovati stopped giving her Alec's blood and returned to giving her the blood from the IV bags.

Alec caressed Nicole's face softly. "Is she okay?" he asked, worried that she would turn despite the girl's words.

Father Rovati shrugged his shoulders. "As far as I can tell she will live, and there are no signs that she will turn, but *why?*" The priest eyed Alec curiously.

Alec shrugged. "I don't have all the answers. That is why I came here ... to seek answers. The only explanation I can offer is that she is the daughter of an immortal."

"Who was on the phone? That is the person that told you how to save her."

"I don't know. She said that she had a message from Nicole."

Shock and disbelief entered the priest's eyes.

"Call the number back," Dash suggested. "And do you think you can see fit to untie me yet? That is unless you still plan to kill me."

Alec's eyes narrowed with suspicion. "Why did you bother to save her? And why didn't you kill us?" he asked the priest.

Rovati frowned. "She is human, it was my duty to do what I could for her ... and she was with you. I suspect that you are different, and maybe even important in preventing a vampire infestation."

"And you just happen to have blood with you?" Alec arched one brow.

"You do not fight vampires without bringing a supply of blood with you," Father Rovati pointed out.

"Untie him," Rovati directed the order to his companions.

The priest's two companions did as they were told without comment.

For the first time, Alec took notice of the men. To most, the slayers would have appeared to be the average everyday people. Maybe even someone you might meet while having coffee in a café, but Alec knew better. These men were professional vampire hunters. He'd met their kind many times.

Father Rovati was no longer paying attention to the others in the room. He was checking Nicole's vital signs. "I think she is comatose," he told them.

"Shouldn't we like ... get her to a hospital or something?" Dash asked, kneeling down beside her.

Just then the phone rang again and Alec flipped it open to answer it. Suspecting that it was the same caller, he put it on speakerphone so that everyone in the room could hear the conversation.

"Hello."

"Nicole is still with me," the girl told him.

"Who is this?" he asked.

"I am Sarah ... Nicole's sister."

At first Alec was too shocked to say anything, but he quickly recovered as a torrent of questions stormed through his mind. "What do you mean she is still with you? We brought her back."

"But she is in a coma ... right?"

"Yes," Alec told her.

"Then she is still separated from her body. I can communicate with those who are between worlds ... or on the other side," she explained.

"Well what can we do for her?" Alec didn't care how, or why the girl knew what she knew. All that mattered to him was Nicole's recovery.

After a long silence Sarah told him, "Don't take her to a hospital. Bring her to New Orleans. I might be able to help her."

"How do we know that you are not working with Omar?" Dash asked loudly.

"You don't, but keep in mind that they are hunting me too."

"So what then? What do we do when we get her to New Orleans?" Alec asked.

Again there was a short silence before Sarah answered. "Nicole is telling me that you should take her to Donavan. I will meet you there."

The line went dead and Alec looked to the priest. "How can we get her back there?"

"I can use a private jet to take her back. Of course it would be too risky for the two of you to travel. It will be light soon."

Alec was disturbed by the idea of these vampire hunters taking Nicole and leaving him behind, but he did not see where there was much choice. He and Dash could take the first flight out of Rome when night returned.

"Okay," Alec nodded.

"But what about the book you came for?" Father Rovati's smile was hard, but not really malicious.

"It will have to wait for another time," Alec told him.

* * * *

Sarah ended the call and turned to Darrien. "We have to get to New Orleans as soon as possible."

Darrien stared at her. "Who was that on the phone and what's going on?"

"Something's happened to my sister, and I need to get to her," Sarah explained, stepping closer to Darrien so she could wrap her arms around his neck.

"I'm still confused," he said, shaking his head.

"She died for a short time, and during that time she came to me and asked for my help." Sarah got on her tiptoes and kissed him lightly on the lips "One of my talents is that I can communicate with the dead."

"You failed to mention this before," Darrien frowned.

"It just never came up." Sarah told him with a sly smile. "I am entitled to a few secrets of my own you know."

"You should hurry." Nicole interrupted the moment, but her voice was weaker now that part of her soul had returned to her body.

"I will. We'll get there as soon as we can," Sarah said, turning away from Darrien.

"You are talking to her now?" he asked.

"Yes," Sarah nodded.

"But I thought she was in a coma?"

"She is, but when someone is in a coma, a part of their soul can still separate from their body." Sarah was already walking away. "We should get some sleep so that we can get as far as possible tonight. I think we can make it all the way to New Orleans before sunrise."

Darrien smiled. "For someone who has never traveled until recently, you sure have become quite the expert."

Entering the tomb, Sarah grabbed the ragged blanket that they'd brought with them, and curled up in a ball on the ground. Within moments she was asleep.

Disappointed that they would not be making love that night, Darrien lay beside her. Though he sought sleep, the memory of the night's hunt still haunted him.

He had not been feeding as much as he should be, and he was growing weak. Tonight he'd been unable to resist his urges, and he'd fed on a human for the first time in weeks.

He was not troubled because he'd killed his victim. The lady would live, as long as she did not have a reaction to the vampire's venom. He'd been careful not to take too much from her, but he could not banish the memory of her face or the horror in her eyes when she'd realized what he was.

She'd pulled her car to the side of the highway. It was the emergency flashers that caught his attention. As soon as he'd approached the car, he'd seen that she had a flat. The right front tire was blown. She stood near the front of the car - wringing her hands anxiously.

Darrien came out of the darkness. "Is there a problem?" he asked, giving the woman his most charming smile.

At first she'd been cautious - backing away from him. "Flat tire," she explained in a small - uncertain voice.

The battle was won as soon as she peered into his eyes. He pulled her in - disarming her with little effort. The vampire's eyes were the most useful of his weapons. With a simple glance, he could hypnotize his prey, and they would become as compliant as a child. Like the deer that stared into the headlights of an oncoming car, his prey would become paralyzed - unable to run or even think.

This ability had served him well in the past, and it did so again, but Darrien had hesitated to take her life. Instead, he'd taken only the blood he'd needed, and then put the woman back in her car. His conscience nagged at him, and he'd hoped to ease it by changing the woman's tire for her.

What good would that do in the end?

He had broken yet another law of the immortals. He had fed on a human, and then let her live to tell about it. Sure, many wouldn't believe her, but some would. It would get the attention of the vampire hunters, and Omar.

And some people would believe!

The vampire often disguised his victims by tearing out the throat to hide the marks left in the neck. The medical examiner would find it curious that there was little blood left in the victim. Ultimately it would be determined that it was the work of a serial killer with a strange taste for blood. Every once in a while a victim survived, and they would rant about vampires. Of course no one believed, the marks were covered with other injuries.

The woman Darrien had left would still have her marks. He had not added another injury to cover his tracks. Some would believe that the marks were the work of a vampire.

Darrien's thoughts turned to Sarah. It would soon be time to say goodbye to her, but when that time came, could he do it? He could no longer picture an existence without her, and there was always the possibility that she would not let him leave. Sarah now had full possession of Caroline's memories and emotions. She had vowed not to be parted from him again.

Suddenly it occurred to him what he must do. It was the only way that he could save her from the pain that his love would bring to her.

Darrien wrapped his arm around Sarah and spent a few moments simply enjoying the sound of her breathing while she slept peacefully. He was thankful that she had returned to him as she had promised, but at the same time, the pain of what he must do was overwhelming. He would have much preferred a cold - emotionless existence, to the agonizing torment of being separated from the one person that made it possible for him to feel anything at all.

* * * *

The small boy ran through the sprinklers, squealing with delight when the water sprayed his face. Like many children, for this boy a hot summer day was a day made just for playing in the water. Finding relief from the heat was just another way to enjoy life. His fair skin was burnt from the sun, but he didn't seem to notice.

It occurred to Sarah that she shouldn't be standing in front of this boy's house to begin with. She was asleep - somewhere on the road to New Orleans. But here she was - watching as the boy soaked himself with the spray of the sprinkler.

Suddenly he seemed to notice her watching him. With a lopsided grin on his face, he walked to where she stood on the sidewalk.

"Thanks for saving my sister."

Sarah shook her head in confusion. "Who is your sister?"

"Nicole."

"Oh ... she's my sister too," Sarah told him, reaching down to ruffle his wet hair.

"I know."

"But she's still very sick," Sarah frowned.

"You know what to do," he said, winking at her.

Sarah laughed, but then a deep sadness came over her. What happened to this small boy that he should be among the dead? Sarah realized that she was dreaming, and that it was no ordinary dream. Nicole's brother was communicating with her through her dream.

Suddenly she felt a tingling sensation on her skin. When she looked down, she could see the boy's hand resting on her arm. "Nicki is so sad. She thinks it was her fault but it wasn't. You'll help her feel better, won't you?"

In that instant Sarah was consumed with a grief so crushing that nothing she had ever felt before even compared. She was feeling her sister's pain, and her loss.

"Won't you?" he asked again.

"Yes, I will do what I can," Sarah told him, her heart crying out in pain. More than anything, she wanted to wrap her arms around this child and bring him back into the world of the living.

"Tell Nicki that the tangled serpent represents the truth that she searches for." The boy's words echoed through her head, before dying away.

Sarah jumped up, her heart racing so fast that she could hear the blood pounding in her ears.

"A bad dream?" Darrien asked, pulling her into his arms.

Sarah shook her head. "No not really … but it was a strange dream."

"You should try to get some more sleep. Nightfall is still an hour or more away."

"Does the term tangled serpent mean anything to you?" she asked.

"No … should it?" he asked.

Sarah shrugged. "I don't know. It's probably nothing."

She didn't really believe her own words. When she had these types of dreams, it was for a reason. But until she knew more, she thought it might be better to keep the dream to herself.

Chapter Nineteen

Father Rovati swatted at an insect that persisted in buzzing around his face. Though the sun was setting, the humidity and heat of Louisiana was unbearable for anyone not accustomed to it.

Pulling a handkerchief from his pocket, the priest wiped the perspiration from his forehead. Now he knew why New Orleans was infested with vampires. These creatures needed heat. They had no way of regulating their body temperature. The cold would not kill them, but it would slow them down. It was the reason you would find many more vampires in warmer climates, and so few in places like Alaska. Contrary to popular belief, there were not all that many vampires in Romania, at least not during the cold season. Not that they would not go to colder regions, they just preferred the warmth. The vampire hated extreme temperatures, cold or hot.

The ride from the airport had been comfortable, thanks to the limousine he'd prearranged before leaving Rome. But as soon as he'd left the air-conditioned limo, he'd been hit with a blast of heat.

Staring at the house, Father Rovati was not surprised by its elegance. It was just like Donavan to setup his base of operation in such luxurious surroundings. He'd known the vampire for decades, and had actually tried to kill him once. What he'd discovered was like Alec - Donavan was different.

A vampire was a vampire, he had no doubt about that, but he knew that a few sought redemption - a different way. Though Donavan accepted what he was as the natural order of things, he had a conscience. This was something that Father Rovati found to be different.

It was after his encounter with Donavan that he'd gone in search of the truth, the beginning of the vampire's curse. What he'd found had shaken the very foundation of his faith. At first he'd been devastated, but then he'd realized that nothing was simply black and white, not even the creations of God. There were always shades of gray between black and white. There had to be negative if there was to be a positive. There were those that lived in the light, and then there were those of darkness - the night breed. It was the law of the universe - the law of God.

From behind him he could hear the two men preparing to move Nicole into the house. One of them would carry her while the other held the IV bag. She was no longer getting blood, but it was necessary to give her liquids to keep her from becoming dehydrated.

At first his companions had hesitated to come with him. But he'd managed to convince them that helping these vampires was for the greater good. Vampire hunters could help control the death that was being spread by these creatures, but they could not cure the problem. That would come from within the ranks of the vampires themselves. Rovati felt that this girl would be part of that.

The walk to the front porch took them through a stunning garden of flowers and fountains. A shiver slid down his spine. He could not help but feel revulsion when he thought of the darkness within, and how such a beautiful garden could so easily mask such darkness.

After climbing the large - covered porch, Father Rovati rang the doorbell. A short time later a blond woman answered the door. Right away he recognized her to be human. Before he could introduce himself and explain his visit, the woman's eyes strayed to the limp body that one of the men behind him was holding in his arms.

"Nicole!" she screamed, rushing out the door.

"She is ill," Father Rovati explained. "We must get her inside and into a bed."

"Of course," she said, motioning for them to follow her.

Vicky Trenton led them into an entry hall and by a staircase to a small bedroom on the main floor.

Nicole was placed in a twin bed with an old fashion patchwork quilt. Father Rovati checked her vitals, and then busied himself changing her IV.

"You can wait for me outside," he spoke to his two companions.

"Are you some kind of doctor? What's wrong with her? What's wrong with my daughter?" Vicky asked, as she held her hands together in an effort to keep them from trembling.

"Yes, at one time I was a doctor," he told her. Her question brought forth troubling memories. He'd been working at the hospital and a girl was brought in. She had been on the verge of death. She was dying from loss of blood, and some type of poisoning that he could not identify. There had been fang marks in her neck, and at first he'd believed the wounds to be inflicted by a snake, but he'd been confused about the loss of blood. Then the girl died.

The other medical personnel had left the room. He was updating the girl's medical charts. He'd heard a noise and looked up. The girl began moving - coming back to life. He'd thought it was a miracle - that was until she'd come at him like a rabid animal.

The first thing he'd thought of was that she'd turned into some kind of zombie, as unbelievable as that was. Then he saw her fangs. In that instant he knew the vampire myth was true. The mutation had been too much for her body, and as quickly as she'd reanimated, she fell to the floor dead once again.

This incident led him to the church, and his mission to rid the world of the vampire. That was a long time ago. Now he knew that it was not some hellish curse. No it was much more complicated than that.

"Father!" Vicky tried to get his attention.

The woman's voice chased the memory away. "She has lost a lot of blood, and is comatose," he finally answered.

"Oh no! They got to her didn't they?" Now Vicky's worry had turned into full-blown panic.

Rovati hesitated only a moment before nodding his head. "I must speak with Donavan Ashe."

Vicky's mouth fell open.

"Yes ... I know him, and I know he is here," he told her, his lips twitched as he tried to smile.

Vicky nodded. "Wait here and I will ask him if he'll see you. What's your name?"

"Father Rovati," he told her.

After the woman left, Rovati studied the room. It appeared so normal, but that was just like Donavan Ashe. It was also like him to take a human mate and sire a daughter. He knew now that was the reason that Alec's blood had not turned her. Nicole was the daughter of an ancient. The blood of the ancients ran through her veins, and that gave her a built in immunity to the poison. That wasn't always the way it worked. Some born vampires were very sensitive to the vampire's poison, and could turn quickly. That didn't seem to be the case with Nicole Ashe.

Stepping to the window, he gazed out at the garden. Though the sun was gone, the gardens were beautifully lit, the walkway illuminated by small lanterns. The scent of roses drifted in the open window.

"Well it's my old enemy, the holy slayer. He has come right into the vampire's lair."

Father Rovati turned at the sound of Donavan's voice. While Rovati had aged, the vampire's sinister good looks had remained the same. This did not surprise him, nor did the fact that Donavan still possessed the same dark charisma that was so useful to the vampire when it came to snaring victims.

"Thank you for returning my daughter to me ... and for not killing her," Donavan added, his lips spreading into a cold smile.

"I also did not kill the two vampires that were with her. They will be along shortly."

"Again ... I must thank you for such an unusually generous act." Donavan took a step toward the priest.

Rovati backed away. He still did not trust Donavan completely. "They were searching for the Book of Anu when they were attacked by other vampires, but it was Alec Norwood that fed on her."

Donavan frowned, but said nothing.

"They deprived him of blood, and then locked her in with him. It was strangely cruel and personal."

"I'm afraid that this was the work of my brother, Omar," Donavan told the priest.

"What is going on Donavan?" Rovati asked, a deep scowl on his face. "They were looking for the Book of Anu ... your daughter and that Alec Norwood. You know how dangerous it could be in the wrong hands."

Donavan smiled and lifted his hands in a gesture of helplessness. "She is a wayward child, I'm afraid."

"And Omar?"

"My brother and his followers have disappeared from New Orleans. I have no way of knowing where he is, but you should be aware that he plans a slaughter like none you have ever seen before, and it will happen soon," Donavan added.

"But why? What does he hope to gain?" Rovati was confused. He had come to know the vampire as a dark creature, but one that only fed to survive. Their nature was changing, and he could not understand why.

Donavan shrugged his shoulders. "To rule the immortals ... to rule the humans. Maybe he is seeking retribution for the power given to the wolves? I cannot tell you what is in my brother's mind."

"What do you plan to do about it?"

"Nothing. I cannot go against my own brother ... my own kind." Donavan turned away from the priest to gaze on the still form of his daughter.

"So you plan to let him slaughter a multitude of innocent people?" Rovati asked, astounded by Donavan's seeming indifference.

"That is not what I said," Donavan's voice turned hard. "It will be up to the Light Seekers and the wolves to bring order back to our world. I help by not impeding their efforts."

"Even after what they've done to your daughter?" Rovati's voice shook with anger.

Donavan's eyes rested on Nicole's pale face. "My daughter knew the possible consequence of loving an immortal, but she will come out of this okay. Her destiny was foretold to me by a higher source."

"You are very sure of yourself," Rovati was doubtful. "Maybe it is time to reveal what is in the Book of Anu?"

Donavan shook his head. "No one would believe, not even the immortals. The time will come, but that time is not now."

Before Rovati could say more, the chiming of the doorbell distracted him.

The true darkness of the immortal would soon rear its ugly head. He knew it - he could feel it deep in his bones.

Chapter Twenty

Sarah wore cutoff shorts and a white T-shirt with pink hearts across the front of it. She appeared to be furthest you could get from a vampire or a witch, but she was both. Darrien stood behind her, his hand resting on her shoulder. His nearness offered her protection and support. Sarah wasn't sure which she needed most at that moment.

The woman that answered the door seemed mildly surprised when she saw them, but to her credit she smiled welcomingly. "Can I help you," she asked.

"I've come to see my sister, to see Nicole," Sarah's words were rushed. She was worried. She hadn't heard Nicole whispering to her for hours now. Not since she'd been given direction on where she should go once she and Darrien reached New Orleans.

"Of course. Please come in." Vicky stepped aside so they could enter. "She's in here."

Sarah and Darrien followed the woman into a small room. A man wearing a black shirt and a priest's collar stood near the bedroom window, but Sarah barely noticed him. It was the other man in the room that commanded her attention. His dark eyes were magnetizing. He very much resembled the girl - the phantom that had come to her the night before. This vampire was her father, and Nicole's father.

Sarah's eyes strayed to the girl on the bed. She was still - her face a pale mask of death. Rushing to her sister's bedside, she placed a hand on her forehead. Her sister was burning with fever. She would need to move quickly before Nicole's soul left her body entirely.

"Sarah?" The deep male voice called to her.

Sarah turned to face the vampire that had fathered her.

"Donavan." Sarah's voice was icy and flat. "Where is my mother?"

He shook his head. "I have not seen her since I went away from you both."

"You mean since you left us stranded in a sleazy motel room in Portland?" Sarah spoke the words through clenched teeth, her anger overcoming her common sense.

For a fraction of a moment she saw shock in his eyes.

"Did you think I would not hear the stories?" she asked coldly.

"I did not have a choice. Maybe one day you will see the truth of this." It was the only explanation he offered.

"Maybe ... but I doubt it," Sarah told him before turning back to Nicole.

There was no more time to waste getting to know the father that had left her behind. At least Nicole had made an effort to find her, and it was her life that Sarah was concerned with at the moment.

Before Sarah could think of what she should do to help Nicole, she heard a commotion at the front of the house and a door slamming. A second later, a man rushed into the room. He was wearing a business suit and seemed completely out of place. She found his run of the mill, clean-cut appearance confusing because he was a vampire. This she was sure of, despite the wire rimmed glasses that he wore, but very likely didn't need. A vampire's eyes were never bad. Sarah knew that much.

The vampire went straight to Nicole's bed. "Alec called me from the airport, he and Dash are on their way," he told them. Glancing up at Sarah, the vampire held out his hand. "You must be Sarah," he smiled. "I'm Ethan. I've been searching for you for a long time."

Sarah shook his hand, and decided right away that this was one vampire that she could like, aside from Darrien.

For the first time Sarah noticed Jeanie in the bedroom doorway, and she ran to her aunt's side. "Thank God you are okay. Darrien told me that someone thrashed the house."

Jeanie waved away Sarah's worry like she always did. "They were just throwing a tantrum … that's all. I'm sure they were very angry to find that you had slipped away right under their noses," she laughed.

"Oh … and Taylor sends his love," Jeanie added with a wink.

Sarah didn't miss the look of distress on Darrien's face. She was sure her aunt had done it purposely, but she chose to ignore her aunt's reference to Taylor.

"We have to do something for Nicole," Sarah told her aunt.

"I know … and we will, but first we need space to work. We'll need enough room to lay her on the floor, and to surround her with candles."

"We can clear out the parlor," Donavan spoke up.

* * * *

Nicole lay on the hardwood floor, encircled by white candles. Sarah knelt beside her, but the rest of the group stood outside the circle. Jeanie had told her what to do, but her aunt could not help. The magic would be far more powerful if a blood relative performed the ritual.

From the darkness beyond the candlelight, Sarah was aware of Alec's anxiety. Ethan and Dash were restraining her sister's lover by force. When he'd arrived, he'd gone straight to Nicole's side. They had been unable to talk him into letting go of her hand, so that Sarah could do what she had to do. It had taken three of them to pull him away from Nicole.

Sarah chanted a spell of life, as she used mint oil to draw a star on Nicole's head. Her hands shook with uncertainty, her doubts taunted her. She was after all - a novice witch. Could she really expect to pull this off?

Pushing the self-doubt from her mind, Sarah cleared her thoughts and concentrated on the task at hand. She picked up her crystal dagger, placing the handle against Nicole's forehead, with the blade positioned toward the ceiling.

"Zaltar! I summons you now!" Sarah called loudly.

The dagger began to glow. At first the blue light was dim, but it slowly brightened.

"I summons the power of earth ... fire ... air ... and water. I call to the spirits that reside in the north ... the south ... the east ... the west. Breathe life back into her lungs. Give voice to her words, and chase away the shadow of death!"

The light emanating from the dagger grew so bright that Sarah was had to use her hand to protect her eyes, but then the light changed into brilliant prisms of color so breathtaking that there was no mistaking it for anything other than magic. When the light faded, a white mist gathered above Nicole's head. Like ghostly fingers, the mist crawled over her body - finding its way into her nose and mouth - entering her head through her ears.

When the smoky mist began to retreat, it moved to Sarah - gathering at her shoulder. The mist darkened until it was completely black, and then it transformed into a raven.

While the raven rested on Sarah's shoulder, she knelt closer to her sister. "Nicole ... can you hear me?"

Nicole's eyes fluttered open and she stared at Sarah, the confusion evident.

"Do you remember me?" Sarah asked.

Nicole shook her head. "No ... maybe. I don't know."

"That's okay," Sarah smiled. "It's not unusual for people to lose their memory of the other side."

"What do you mean ... the other side?" Nicole tried to sit up, but the effort seemed too much for her.

"You were very close to death," Sarah told her.

"Nicole!" Alec called from across the room. Breaking away from Dash and Ethan, Alec went to where Nicole lay on the floor and knelt by her side.

"Can you ever forgive me?" Alec choked on his words.

Nicole reached up to touch his face. "There is nothing to forgive. I would do it all over again."

Alec shook his head. "No! You will never risk your life for me again."

Nicole's only response was a strained smile. She then closed her eyes and drifted into sleep.

Vicky stepped forward to take her daughter's hand. "Let's get her to bed. She is still weak and needs her rest."

Sarah felt a twinge of jealousy that her sister should enjoy the love of a mother, while she had been denied that love for so long. Shamed by her thoughts, Sarah pushed them out of her head and reached out to grab Vicky's hand.

"I saw your son in a dream. He is happy and at peace. He is always near you and Nicole."

Tears crept into Vicky's eyes. "Thank you," she said, clearing her throat. "You should tell Nicole this when she is well. She will want to hear about her brother."

* * * *

Sarah sat on a marble bench, enjoying the garden and the cool evening breeze. It had been two days since Nicole had woken, and she was quickly regaining her strength. Sarah had spent many hours getting to know her sister, and filling her in on what had happened while she was comatose.

The sound of footsteps on the stone walkway intruded on the peaceful solitude she'd found in the garden. Donavan approached her, but Sarah refused to acknowledge him.

"Sarah ... do you mind if I sit here?" he asked.

Sarah shrugged.

"You have not spoken to me since the night you arrived. I believe we have much to talk about."

"Not really," Sarah told him as she stood to leave.

"Please don't go. Talk with me," Donavan spoke up before she could walk away.

Taking a deep breath, Sarah returned to sitting on the bench next to him. "What do you have to say to me that you couldn't have said years ago?" she asked.

"I have three daughters, and I love them all equally. You must understand Sarah ... I will not be the cause of harm coming to them. And I will not bring this curse of my existence onto the women that I have loved," he tried to explain.

"What do you mean?" Sarah was confused.

"Your mother ... she would not accept what she was. Beth wanted me to turn her into what I am, but I refused." Donavan grew silent for a long time before he continued.

"I knew that she loved me and would have done anything for me ... even give up her existence as a human. I couldn't let her do that. I loved her in my own way, and did not want her to live like I have had to live. Then there was you. I knew she could not be the mother that you needed, if she were to live as an immortal."

"Well she wasn't that anyway." Sarah's words were full of bitterness.

Sarah didn't resist when Donavan took her hand in his. "For that I am so very sorry."

Sarah closed her eyes in an effort to hide her pain. "Jeanie was good to me. She was always there when I needed her."

"Yes, and I am eternally grateful to her for the love that she has given you ... though I know she still disapproves of me," Donavan added with a smile.

"So what do you think happened to my mother?" she asked, her heart softening slightly toward her father.

"I believe that she went in search of a vampire that would turn her. The fact that she never returned for you tells me that she found what she was looking for, and he brought her death, instead of the eternal life that she wanted."

Tears stung Sarah's eyes. Her mother had been so beautiful and so full of life. It was difficult to imagine that she was really gone. She had always believed that her mom would come back for her someday. She had fantasized about it as a child - daydreaming about what it would be like.

Her mother would walk up the drive of the old Fabre mansion, and with that beautiful smile on her lips, she would open her arms to Sarah. On that day, her mother would give her the biggest hug ever.

But that day had never come, and now she knew that it never would.

Her father reached up and gently wiped away the tears that were flowing down her cheeks. "I do have some information about her."

Sarah held her breath, waiting for him to continue.

"I asked Ethan to see if he could track down Beth's movements after she left you in Sutter Point. He was able to trace her to Wyoming. That was about ten years ago. It was the last place she was known to be."

"That doesn't make any sense." Sarah drew her brows together in confusion. "If she were searching for vampires, wouldn't she have come here to New Orleans ... or maybe someplace like Romania?"

"You would think ... but that is what we've been able to uncover so far."

Sarah stood up. "I'm tired ... I think I'll go to bed early tonight," she told him. The truth was that she just needed some time alone to digest what he'd told her, and to come to terms with her mother's fate.

Sarah started to walk away, but paused at the sound of Donavan's voice.

"Do not make the same mistake as your mother Sarah. An immortal cannot be what you need ... not really."

* * * *

Though the night breeze drifted through the bedroom window, she still felt as if she were suffocating.

"Sarah!" a voice called to her from outside.

Sarah left her bed to go to the window. Darrien stood in the garden below, motioning for her to come out.

"What are you doing down there?" she asked.

Darrien put a finger up to his lips. "Don't be so loud. Come out and play for a while."

Sarah felt her heart race as she anticipated what type of playing he wanted to do. Darrien had made himself scarce since their arrival in New Orleans. She'd seen him only once since that night, and even that was only for a short moment at her bedroom window. There had been only time enough for a quick kiss, before they'd heard someone coming.

Darrien was aware of Donavan's feelings about his relationship with Sarah, but she hoped that her father's disapproval would not matter. It shouldn't matter. Not after he'd been absent for most of her life.

"I'll be down in a minute," she told him, blowing Darrien a kiss before leaving the window.

Sarah turned from the window and froze. Gina blocked the door. The ghastly vision sent shards of fear into Sarah's heart. Weeds clung to her wet hair. Her face was swollen and gray - just as it had been on the day they had pulled her body from the water.

"Go away Gina!" Sarah closed her eyes, hoping that when she opened them again, the ghost would be gone.

When Sarah looked again, Gina was still there.

"What do you want?" Sarah asked, angry that her friend would not let her be. All of these years she had not heard so much as a whisper from her friend, and now Gina was haunting her - popping up around every corner.

"Death is painful … but the pain does go away."

Sarah heard Gina's voice in her head, but before she had time to contemplate the meaning of her words, she vanished.

Baffled, Sarah left the room. Tonight she needed the solace of Darrien's arms more than ever. She found him waiting for her in the garden, and she all but flew into his embrace.

"Are you okay?" he asked, startled by her behavior.

"Yes," Sarah whispered. Getting on her tiptoes she placed a quick kiss on his lips. "I've just missed you … that's all."

Darrien smiled. "Have you ever made love on a riverbank?"

Sarah shook her head.

"Well now you will." Darrien wrapped his arms around her waist and they rose up into the darkness. A moment later Sarah could see the glistening black water of the Mississippi below them.

Slowly they descended from the sky. Darrien gently laid her back in the tall grass of the riverbank. His eyes were alight with his hunger for her, but that hunger was softened by love and something else ... sadness. Sarah saw sadness in his eyes.

She opened her mouth to ask him what was wrong, but before she could say a word, Darrien silenced her with a deep kiss. His tongue danced with hers - caressing the inside of her mouth, while his hands stroked the inside of her thighs.

Darrien pulled away and whispered in her ear. "Going two nights without you has been torture."

"Hmm ... I know what you mean," she told him as her fingers sought out the button of his pants. With deft movement, Sarah released his stiff flesh from the confines of his pants, and wrapped her hand around him.

"You move so quickly," he panted.

Sarah giggled. "I can't help myself. You've neglected me too long," she told him as she gently pulled on his erection. She loved the way his body trembled as his hunger for her grew.

"Witch"

"And I'm very wicked," she laughed.

As he stared into her eyes, Sarah felt herself falling into the fire she saw within them.

"Do you remember everything now? Do you remember being Caroline?" he asked in low voice.

Sarah nodded. "I do remember. I remember making love with you in field of wildflowers ... beneath the sun."

"You would never be able to do that with me again," he told her, his voice cracking with emotion and the need that was overwhelming him.

"I don't care," she told him, lifting her head so that she could kiss his lips.

Darrien lost it then. His mouth devoured hers in a hungry -
demanding kiss. His hands lifted her nightgown so that he could
get to her panties. Slowly he slid them off and when she was free
of them, his hand went between her thighs to gently spread her
legs.

Sarah felt her legs grow weak, and she began to shake as she
anticipated the moment he would enter her.

"I want you to bite me while we are making love," she
gasped, fighting to get her breathing under control.

Darrien growled and she felt his fangs pierce her neck. In
that same instant, she felt his hard flesh penetrating her. The
moist heat between her legs erupted into a raging blaze of
passion. The feeling of him feeding on her, as he moved within
her, was so erotic that she was almost instantly pulled into an
earth-shattering orgasm.

Sarah howled with delight as she savored the feeling of him
thrusting into her frantically, consumed by his mind-numbing
need. As she felt him spill his seed within her, she wrapped her
legs around him, and let him bring her to that place of
unbelievable pleasure, once again.

She felt some pain when he withdrew his fangs from her
flesh, but she was soothed by the feeling of his tongue licking
away the droplets of blood that still flowed from the wound.

"I love you," he whispered in her ear.

"Not as much as I love you." Sarah smiled, content with life
for the first time that she could remember. It wasn't perfect, but
with Darrien by her side, it was as close to perfect as it had ever
been.

Chapter Twenty-One

Sarah stared at her reflection in the mirror. Her eyes fixed on the purple bruising around the bite marks on her neck. She cursed the heat that prevented her from wearing a turtleneck sweater that would help to hide the marks.

There was nothing she could do but position her long hair around her neck so that it would hide the bite. It wasn't so much that she was afraid of Donavan, at least not for herself. She just wasn't sure what might happen to Darrien if her father saw the marks on her.

Sarah glanced at the red numbers displayed on the digital alarm clock on her bedside table. It was nearly time to go downstairs. Ethan had called a meeting for 10:00 PM and he'd asked that they all be there.

Though she was still getting to know everyone, she found them all likable in different ways. Ethan was amusing because he tried too hard to be mortal. Dash was fun to be with. No matter how down you were feeling, he could always find some way to make you smile. Then there was Nicole. Her sister was everything she'd ever imagined that she would be, and more. Sarah almost didn't know how to react to having a big sister around.

From the murmur of voices she could hear as she descended the stairs, it sounded as if everyone had arrived. When Sarah stepped into the parlor, her eyes scanned the room looking for Darrien. She saw Dash, Alec, her sister and the priest. Aunt Jeanie was even there. It appeared everyone was present but him.

This didn't surprise her too much. His interest in the Light Seekers was limited to her. He didn't really believe that they would ever be successful. He never said this to her, but she could feel it coming from him whenever she spoke of the Place of Light, or the secrets that the ancients were hiding. He just didn't believe.

When everyone had found a place to sit, Ethan stood up and faced them. "We have a few different things that we need to discuss tonight."

Sarah felt a twinge of alarm when Ethan scanned the crowd, but his eyes quickly skipped over her. He seemed different somehow. Ethan's face actually had some color to it. He was nowhere near as pale as usual.

"First … I am sure everyone is aware that Omar and his vamps are gone. It appears as if they have disappeared off of the face of the earth, but don't be fooled. This doesn't mean that he has hightailed it. What it means is that something very serious is getting ready to go down … so we better be ready for it.

"I know this is basically a vampire problem and not everyone here is a vampire, but we all have something in common. We are all targets of these renegade vamps."

"How are we suppose to be ready for something, if we don't know what that something is?" Jeanie spoke up.

Ethan shook his head. "I don't know. Just keep an eye open at all times."

"What else is going on?" Nicole asked. "I know you Ethan. You wouldn't call everyone together just to tell us about something that you know we have already guessed."

She was sitting on the couch next to Alec. Nicole's dislocated shoulder was in a sling to keep her arm stationary. She had a blanket wrapped around her. Even in the stifling heat of the day, Nicole complained of being cold. Sarah still feared that there was a chance that her sister might turn.

"Dash and I have been talking, and we decided that it was time that we tried to cross into the Place of Light," he told them.

"How are you going to do this when you don't even know how to get to this place?" Alec scoffed at the idea.

"I have been doing a lot of research on the subject, and I think I have a general idea of where the gateways are," Ethan told them. "What I've found matches closely to what Dash experienced. I think that maybe we could send someone over there. They could check it out."

"Who is going to do this?" Nicole asked.

Dash stood up and smiled. "That would be me. I would be an ambassador of sorts. You know ... I would kind of just slip over there and have a bit of a talk with whoever's in charge."

Nicole shook her head. "No ... no way."

Father Rovati cleared his throat to get their attention. "To tell you the truth, I can't even believe that I am sitting here listening to all of this. I have spent my life hunting vampires, and now I am at some kind of a vampire meeting. To top that off ... I am listening to some strange idea about going to a place that very likely doesn't exist, except for in legends."

"It does exist," Donavan interceded. "But it is foolish to think that any of us would go there and live to return. It is the realm of the wolves."

"I don't know. The wolves don't seem like such a bad sort," Dash said, cocking his head to one side.

Donavan's smile was chilling. "Need I remind you that we are not talking about a lone vampire going into a den of wolves ... but an entire kingdom of wolves? We are talking about a species that has been our enemy since the dawn of time."

"I have to agree with Dash. They don't seem so bad," Sarah told them.

"And now my daughter is an expert on the wolves," Donavan glowered at her.

"Well no ... but I know a little about them," Sarah defended herself.

"As do I." Nicole pushed the blanket from her shoulders and got to her feet. At first she swayed a little, but Alec was there to steady her.

"It would be foolish for you to go there. Lex told me that only one vampire has ever gone to this place and survived. I don't want you to go Dash ... not alone," Nicole added.

"It doesn't make sense for everyone to risk their lives," Dash told her. "And besides ... I am so tired of the darkness it doesn't really matter to me anymore."

"No Dash," Nicole shook her head. "We need you here. There's still a lot to do. We have to find my youngest sister."

Dash gave her a sad smile. "You don't need me for that. Ethan's your man for those types of things."

Nicole was ready to fling out more objections when Ethan held up his hand. "We will accompany him, at least to the gateway."

Nicole searched the faces of the people that were gathered. "Where is Lex? Why isn't he here? He would tell you how foolish this is."

"Lex had some urgent business to attend to. He sends his regards, and regrets that he could not stay," Ethan told them.

Sarah didn't miss the frown on Aunt Jeanie's face at the news that Lex was gone. If she didn't know better, she would think that her aunt was actually falling for the wolf man.

"So if there are no more objections ... we will make plans to leave for Wyoming within the next couple of weeks. We should leave as soon as Nicole is ready to travel," Ethan told them.

Nicole turned away, saying no more.

Sarah's stomach knotted up when Ethan's eyes came to rest on her. Her sixth sense had known from the moment she'd walked into the room that something was wrong - something was terribly wrong.

Donavan jumped in, before Ethan could say anything. "Sarah, will you come out to the garden so that we may speak with you in private?"

A lumped was forming in her throat. All of the sudden she didn't want to know. As long as she didn't know, she could pretend everything was okay. She wanted to scream at them to leave her alone - to keep whatever they wanted to say to themselves. But instead she nodded, following her father and Ethan into the garden.

"When was the last time that you saw Darrien?" her father asked.

"Last night ... why?"

"Did the two of you fight ... have a falling out maybe?"

Sarah shook her head. "No not at all."

Donavan placed a hand on her shoulder and led her to the marble bench. "Sit Sarah," he told her.

Sarah did as he asked, but her eyes never left his face. She tried to read his expression, but he was too good at hiding his feelings.

"This morning he brought this letter to Ethan and asked that it be given to you." Donavan held out an envelope.

"And as the sun came up," Donavan continued. "Darrien walked into it."

Sarah shook her head. "I don't understand. What are you saying?"

"Darrien destroyed himself," her father told her.

Everything went black. For a fraction of a moment Sarah could see or hear nothing. She felt someone's hands on her, holding her up.

"Sarah!" Donavan called her name, pulling her back from the dark tunnel that she was falling into. Finally her father's face came into focus.

"No! I don't believe it. He just came to me last night," she cried.

"I'm sorry. I know he was someone that you cared about deeply," Donavan tried to comfort her.

Sarah shook her head frantically. "You did something to him," she accused. "You didn't want us together so you had him destroyed!"

"This is not true," Donavan denied.

"I saw what he did with my own eyes," Ethan told her. "He just walked outside as the sun was coming up."

"And ... and you did nothing to stop him?" Sarah's sobbing made it difficult for her to speak.

"Of course I did. I went out after him." Ethan removed his jacket and rolled up the sleeves of his shirt. There were blisters up and down his arms and on his hands.

Now that she thought about it, she realized that she hadn't seen his hands while he was talking to them in the parlor. He'd kept them in the pockets of his jacket.

"Your face isn't burned," she stated.

"I keep a ski mask nearby just in case I need to go out quickly, but I did burn some anyway."

Sarah buried her face in her hands and cried. How could he have done this? How could he have left her just when she was beginning to find happiness?

"Where is he? Darrien deserves a proper burial," she cried.

"I don't know," Ethan told her. "I contacted the police and asked the people that I usually work with if they would keep an eye out for a body, but so far there hasn't been one. I also asked Lex if he would look for him. That is why he isn't here tonight."

"Well he has to be somewhere. He couldn't just disappear, could he?"

"He will turn up sooner or later," Donavan reassured her. "Then we will do what you believe to be right."

"I don't just believe it to be right, I *know* it is the right thing to do," she responded, her emotion making it impossible to think straight. "I knew him as a child. His family believed in heaven, and in God. Darrien did too … once."

Both Donavan and Ethan looked at her in bewilderment. "What do you mean you knew him as a child?"

Sarah shook her head. "It doesn't matter. It never really did, I guess."

"Why don't you go lie down now?" Donavan urged. "This has been draining for you."

Sarah stared at the letter she held in her hand. She needed no more encouragement. She would experience her last moments with Darrien through the words in his letter, but it was all that she had left of him.

Nodding to her father and Ethan, Sarah left the garden and ran up to her room. Shutting the door behind her, she fell into her bed and let the tears come. She kept seeing him on his horse - beneath the sunshine. The way he'd smiled at her, so tenderly but so full of mischief. That was back when he was mortal, and could be in the light. It was when she was Caroline, instead of Sarah.

Sarah's body shook uncontrollably as she wept.

Now he would be in the light - that light that so many of the immortals craved. But Sarah - she was in a place of darkness that she may never emerge from. There had not been a hint of what was to come from the spirit world.

But that was not really true. Gina had warned her about the pain of death, but Sarah had assumed that the ghost had been referring to her own death - the process of death - not Darrien's death.

Finally her tears slowed. Sarah left her bed to go into the bathroom that was adjoined to her room. She splashed cold water on her tear-swollen eyes, and then dried her face.

It was several moments before she felt calm enough to confront the letter that he'd left. Finally she picked it up from the bed where it waited for her. Taking a deep breath, Sarah carefully opened the envelope and pulled out a single piece of paper.

Sarah My Love

Yes I am calling you Sarah and not Caroline. You are Sarah now, and I love Sarah. Maybe one day you will forgive me for what I am about to do. Please believe that what I do, I am doing for you. No, maybe it isn't just for you. I just cannot live without you. Not again. For over two hundred years I have lived in the darkness, wanting to feel your warmth and see the light in your eyes. I don't think that I am strong enough to go through an eternity without you.

I brought you death once. I will not do so again. I know you don't believe that this would happen, that I would be responsible for your death again, but even if this is true, eventually you will die. You must. It is inevitable for all mortals. This time when you die, I will be waiting for you on the other side. Even though I am gone, my love for you will live on forever. Always remember that.

I love you Forever

Darrien

Again her tears came. This time they were not just tears of grief, but also tears of anger. How could he have been so selfish and so thoughtless? He had released himself from pain, only to bring it to her.

There was a knock at her door.

"Sarah!" Aunt Jeanie called to her from the hall.

The door opened and Jeanie came in the room. She walked to the bed and sat next to Sarah. There were tears in her aunt's eyes.

"I am so sorry baby girl," Jeanie told her as she gathered Sarah into her arms.

Chapter Twenty-Two

In the fading light of dusk, the headlights did little to illuminate the road. Even with the keen sight of the wolf, the dirt road could be hazardous and difficult to navigate. Though there was still some light in the sky, the woods were dark and ominous. His aging eyes were not what they once were.

Spotting his destination up ahead, Lex pulled off to the side of the road. He switched the ignition off, but left the headlights on. When he opened the car door to get out, he was surprised at how cool it was. Though it was only late summer, the night air already had a chill to it.

With the spare set of keys that he kept in his pocket, Lex opened the trunk. He pulled out a flashlight and switched it on. The beam of the light was directed toward what at first appeared to be a pile of green wool blankets, but at closer inspection, it was obvious that the blankets were wrapped around something.

Lex leaned over and pulled the form from the trunk, flinging it over his shoulder. At least he could be thankful that his strength was not fading like his eyesight. With the light directed in front of him, Lex made his way along the steep path that would take him further up the mountain.

After several moments of climbing, Lex finally came to a gaping black hole in the side of the mountain. It was one of many caves that could be found along the Wind River mountain range. Though he pointed the flashlight into the opening, it could not penetrate the darkness in the cave. He entered regardless. If there were a bear hidden by that darkness, he would deal with that threat when the time came. Right now he wanted to relieve himself of the burden he carried on his shoulder.

Lex didn't stop in the main cavern, but took another tunnel to a smaller cavern, deeper within the cave. He then placed the wrapped body on the earthen floor. For a long time he just stood there, staring at the heap he had deposited on the ground. Finally he knelt down and began unwrapping the form hidden within the blankets.

The body was burned badly. Wherever the skin was exposed was nothing but a mass of oozing blisters. The skin on one side of his face almost appeared to be melted plastic.

He left the cave but returned shortly, his arms laden with supplies. Lex then took some scissors from one of the bags that he'd been carrying and began cutting the clothes away from Darrien's body. When the clothes were cut away from the burned flesh, he then took a jug of water and began pouring it over Darrien's burns.

Lex shook his head. "You foolish boy."

He next opened a cooler and grabbed a plastic IV bag full of blood. He attached a tube to the bag and placed the other end of the tube in Darrien's mouth, so that the blood would slowly drip.

Stepping back from the body, Lex could not believe what he was doing. Helping the vampires was one thing, but this was really going above and beyond the call of duty.

Why was he doing it?

It was for Sarah. She was important to the big picture, and Darrien was important to her.

Getting the blood hadn't been easy. He'd had to steal it from a blood bank, and was nearly caught.

Keeping Darrien out of the sun was essential, but there was no way to do that in New Orleans. Not without putting him in some filthy crypt. Lex had decided he would take him away from New Orleans - away from the threat of other vampires and the prying eyes of the humans.

The boy had problems, and even if he lived, he may decide to find another way to end his existence.

Lex shook his head again. He had a lot of work ahead of him to take care of this problem.

* * * *

Sarah eyed the black vehicle that Ethan had parked in front of Donavan's Garden District house. It was definitely out of place in this neighborhood. Truthfully, it would look to be out of place just about anywhere.

The vehicle was a large van that had been converted into something else. What that something else was, Sarah wasn't sure. The windshield and the front door windows were darkly tinted. It had no other windows.

"So much for blending in," Sarah commented dryly.

"It is exactly what we need," Ethan told her and the others that were gathered at the curb to see it. "We will not be limited to only traveling during the night. With this piece of machinery, we can travel whenever we want. During the day, those of us that can't be in the light will remain in the back, and one of you girls can drive."

"How do you keep the light out of the back?" Alec was unconvinced.

Ethan walked around to the back of the van and opened the doors. A light came on so that they could see inside. On one side of the van was a couch, on the other side there was a flat screen computer monitor, hanging from the wall of the van. On the floor was a small refrigerator. The front of the van was completely closed off from the back with a sliding metal door.

"You see. There is no way for light to get in here unless the doors are opened. There are cameras hooked up around the outside of the van and in the driver's area so that we can see what's going on from back here. We can also communicate through an intercom system that I've installed."

"Very innovative," Dash smiled. "Do you think we could like … hook up a video game system to that monitor?"

"It's that kind of frivolous thinking that is going to get you someday," Donavan's voice took them by surprise. He had not come out with the group to look at the vehicle as he'd been closed up in his study for hours with Father Rovati. The two of them had been in a heated discussion about something that the others weren't permitted to know about.

Dash shrugged. "It was just an idea. You know ... break the boredom of the road."

Ethan pointed to the refrigerator. "We can carry an emergency supply with us ... and soda to if you want," he said, looking at Nicole and Sarah.

"So when do we leave?" Sarah asked, but without much excitement.

"Tomorrow night. That should give everyone a chance to be ready," Ethan told them.

"Well Dash," Nicole put an arm around the vampire's shoulder. "It looks like you finally get to go back to Wyoming."

Though Nicole was trying to act cheerful, it was evident that she was still upset about Dash's decision.

"Yes, I've waited a long time for this," he said with a sad smile.

As the others walked away to return to the house, Jeanie grabbed Sarah's hand. "Wait ... I wanted to have a word with you."

Sarah stopped and stared at her aunt. "Is everything okay?" she asked.

"I don't know. Is it?"

Sarah shrugged her shoulders. "I'm okay ... considering."

Jeanie was doubtful. "I feel as if the real Sarah has retreated into herself. You are so hard ... so cold now."

"It's only been two weeks. I'm sure I'll get over it sooner or later," Sarah frowned.

The truth was that at the beginning she'd been unable to accept the reality of Darrien's death. Even with the letter he'd left her, it just seemed so impossible - so unreal. As the days went by, she did begin to accept his death as real, and to accept the fact that he was just gone. Darrien was no longer a part of her life, and never would be again.

Acceptance had not brought her relief from the pain, nor did it ease her anger. She almost felt as if Sarah no longer existed. She was just a shell, going through the motions of life.

Jeanie was watching her, pulling Sarah's thoughts from her head.

"I wish you wouldn't do that," Sarah told her.

"I'm worried about you. I know you cared about him, but you still have your whole life ahead of you. Please don't let me lose you like I did your mother."

Sarah forced a smile. "Really … I'll be okay."

Jeanie didn't seem to believe her, but instead of pressuring her further, she changed the subject. "Tomorrow morning I'm leaving to go back to Sutter Point."

"Why?" Sarah was shocked by this new development.

Her aunt shrugged. "I don't really belong here. I know that this is something that you must do, but I just think that I could be more useful back home."

"Are you sure that it isn't because a certain gentleman is no longer here?" Sarah asked with a smile. It was the first time in two weeks that her smile was truly genuine. She was happy that her aunt was feeling the first pangs of romance.

"Don't be ridiculous," Jeanie scoffed.

"It's okay auntie," Sarah told Jeanie as she grabbed her hand and started walking toward the front porch. "I'm sure there will be plenty of opportunity to meet up with him again."

* * * *

Sarah was sure that the little two-lane highway would go on forever. They'd been traveling for nearly two days with only short stops to sleep for a few hours. On both sides of them were nothing but sagebrush and hills, but in the distance she could make out a mountain range.

The speaker in the dashboard came alive. "This looks familiar," Dash told them. "I think there is a rest stop not far from here. Pull over there."

Nicole leaned forward and pushed the button on the intercom. "Are you sure? The sun isn't completely down yet?"

"Yes. I need to get my bearings," he answered, but a burst of static made it difficult to understand what he was saying.

Sarah shrugged. "Well I guess he wants us to stop anyway." She'd be glad for the opportunity to get out and stretch her legs. Besides, it was Nicole's turn to drive.

Sure enough, Sarah drove two more miles before coming to the sign for the rest stop. It was to her left. Sarah flipped on the blinker and made the turn. Not that she really needed to use the blinker, there hadn't been another car for at least an hour.

Sarah brought the van to a stop near the restrooms. After turning off the engine, she pushed the button to talk to those in back. "Are you sure this is the place?" she asked.

There was an eruption of static from the speaker, but they couldn't hear anything beyond that.

"I can't hear you. I asked if you were sure this is the place?" Sarah tried again.

Again, there was only static. Nicole and Sarah stared at each other.

"Something's wrong!" Nicole said as she was unfastening her seatbelt. "We need to check on them."

Sarah reached out and grabbed Nicole's arm before she could open her door. "Whatever is wrong, you'll only make it worse by opening those doors right now."

Nicole stopped and stared into the western sky where the red sun was slowly setting - too slowly.

"I mean really ... what could be wrong? We've been moving the whole time," Sarah reasoned.

"Well we should make sure the door is still shut," Nicole said as she jumped out of the van.

Sarah followed her sister. The two of them stood behind the van, staring at the closed doors. Sarah could feel her sister fighting the urge to fling those doors open.

"I'm sure he's fine," she tried to reassure Nicole. "It should only be a few more minutes before we can safely open the doors. Maybe you can get one of them on your mobile?" Sarah suggested.

Nicole pulled her phone from her pants pocket. "There's no service."

Sarah checked her phone and she also had no service. This wasn't surprising, considering they were in the middle of nowhere.

Every couple of minutes Nicole peered at the sun. Finally when the last rays faded from the horizon, she went for the doors. As soon as she opened them, Dash, Alec and Ethan stepped out.

Nicole threw her arms around Alec's neck. "You scared the hell out of me. What's wrong with the intercom?" she asked.

Ethan already had a screwdriver in his hand that he'd taken from the luggage compartment on the side of the van.

"I don't know. There was just so much static that we couldn't hear you over it," Ethan answered for Alec as he was climbing back into the van.

"That's what it was like in front," Sarah told them.

Suddenly Ethan stopped what he was doing and looked at them. "Maybe it's because we're close. If you think about it ... if there is a portal there has to be some kind of energy associated with it. That energy could interfere with any type of electronics."

Dash was staring up the road. "We are close ... I remember this place."

"So you saw this guy on this road, miles from any kind of civilization ... and he let you see a vision of the Place of Light?" Alec's skepticism came through in his voice.

"You see ... there you go!" Dash threw his hands in the air. "I knew you never believed me."

"Okay … okay," Nicole stepped in. "So we know that it's probably somewhere around here, but where? What do we do now?"

Ethan was holding a portable GPS in his hand, and was waiting for it to locate them. "This isn't working either."

"I tell you … that little dude was right down the road from here," Dash mumbled.

Nicole held up her hand to silence everyone. "Both times we have had these visions it was done with a medallion, and I am not even sure that what I experienced was real. Anyway, let's not forget that as far as we know, the only people that possess these medallions are the ancients. Has anyone considered what we will do even if we find this portal?"

Dash grinned and pulled something out of his shirt pocket. A golden medallion hung from the chain he held in his hands. Like Donavan's medallion, this one had a crystal in the middle and was surrounded by those strange markings.

"Where did you get that?" Alec asked in a tight voice.

Dash glanced at Nicole. "Do you remember when we were at Castle Arges? Well I found this little beauty sitting on a table right in plain sight."

Nicole gasped. "You took that from Luciano?"

Dash shrugged. "I figured we could make better use of it. This is why I suggested this trip."

"That was foolish," Alec grumbled.

Ethan was just staring at them with his mouth agape. "Do you have any idea who you just stole from … how dangerous he is?"

"Sure, but I did it … not you guys. Besides, I'll be beyond his reach … one way or another," he added with a smile.

"This doesn't solve the problem of where this place is, or even if it is?" Alec pointed out. "I don't know if you realize this, but what Dash and Nicole experienced was a vision. They did not actually go to this place. They both saw it while holding that medallion in their hand. Has it occurred to anyone that there could be something in that crystal that causes hallucinations?"

Nicole shook her head. "Lex and my father claim that it is real. Plus, it is where Lex says that he is originally from."

"But what do we know about this lycan? I mean really. He starts showing up and giving us information. How do we know he isn't leading us into a trap?" It was obvious that Alec was becoming more agitated and troubled by the minute.

"Well he has helped us a lot, especially me," Sarah defended him.

"No matter, we still don't know how to find this place," Alec told them.

"Sarah's psychic. Maybe she can find it," Dash offered.

Sarah shook her head. "It doesn't work that way. I can't pick and choose the information I get. If I were going to get something on the location of this place, I probably would have already."

"Maybe we should do this the old fashion way," Nicole suggested. "We'll ask around and see if anyone knows anything?"

"Right! We are going to ask if anyone knows how to get to another dimension?" Ethan laughed. "They will send the police after us thinking we are a bunch of nuts."

"Do you have a better idea?" Nicole asked.

Suddenly Ethan perked up. "You know … I did bring along my infrared camera. It might pick up any electromagnetic fields in the area."

"Let's try it," Dash told him.

A moment later Ethan had the camera on and was scanning the horizon. As he slowly moved the camera to the east, white filled the digital screen. "I think we have our coordinates," he told them. "There is some major electromagnetic energy coming from that direction." Ethan pointed toward the northeast.

"We're wasting time. Let's get going," Alec told them.

"Wait!" Sarah spoke up. "Before we start moving again I need to use the restroom."

Sarah left the others and started walking toward the restrooms. Thankfully the building had some lighting, but it wasn't very bright. As she got closer, she saw that the side closest to the parking lot housed the men's room. The women's restroom was on the other side of the building - out of sight of the parking lot and her friends.

She hesitated. It was dark, and though there was some light, it wasn't much. Every nerve in her body began to tingle. Something wasn't right. There just seemed to be something out of place or different from a few moments before. That little voice in her head urged her to run back to the van.

But she really needed to use the restroom!

Taking a deep breath, Sarah walked around the building to the women's restrooms and quickly went inside. The bathroom was brightly lit, and the light eased her discomfort some.

Sarah quickly finished and was at the sink washing her hands when she heard a noise by the restroom's entrance. She quietly made her way to the door, and opened it just a crack to see if anyone was out there. There was nothing but buzzing insects near the outside light.

She opened the door wider and stepped out. A quick sprint to the van and it would be all over. She could breathe easy again. Sarah took one step and then froze. Someone was watching her, hidden by the darkness that was just beyond the reach of the light.

There was something very familiar about him. Sarah took a step toward the figure, but was stopped by his words.

"Don't come closer."

The voice was raspy and hollow, but still familiar.

"Darrien," Sarah whispered his name.

"Go away," he barked.

Again Sarah took a step toward him, but the figure turned away from her and fled into the darkness.

"Darrien!" she called after him.

Nicole and the others came around the building. "What's wrong?" her sister asked.

"It was Darrien. He was right here."

"Sarah that's impossible. You know that's impossible." Nicole's voice was sympathetic but firm.

"Well she does see ghosts," Dash offered an explanation. "Do vampires turn into ghosts do you think? I mean when the end finally comes?"

"Dash!" Nicole gave him a look of disapproval.

"Sorry," he said, putting his arm around Sarah. "Maybe it was that burrito you ate?"

Sarah scowled. "It was Darrien. I swear it was. And I don't think he was a ghost. He didn't act like a ghost."

"Ghost or not ... whoever it was is gone now," Alec told her patiently.

Ethan slapped his hands together. "We're wasting time, let's go."

Sarah followed the others to the van. Again Dash put his arm around her. "You know Sarah ... I'm a vampire too. If it wasn't for the fact that I'm getting ready to go away ..."

Nicole swung around to glare at him. "Dash!"

"Sorry," he grinned.

"You're terrible," Nicole scolded.

Chapter Twenty-Three

Back on the highway, Ethan rode in the passenger side seat with his camera pointed out the window. They drove for about two miles before spotting a dirt road that led off in the direction that the camera was picking up the electromagnetic energy.

"Turn off here," Ethan told Nicole.

Nicole hit the breaks, slowing down so that she could make the turn, without rolling the van. "It would have been nice to have a little more warning," she grumbled.

For the next twenty minutes Nicole followed the dirt road, turning off in a different direction whenever Ethan directed her to. The road was getting rocky and difficult to drive on.

"I don't know how much further we can go without damaging the van," she told Ethan.

"It's okay. You can pull off now. We are close."

As soon as the van came to a stop, Ethan jumped out and started walking. "Hey! Wait for us!" Nicole yelled.

Soon they were all following Ethan. Sarah held the flashlight, pointing the beam of light in front of them. They walked only a short distance before coming to the mouth of a large cave.

"The energy is coming from in there," Ethan told them.

Everyone's eyes rested on Dash.

"Are you ready for this?" Ethan asked him.

Dash took the medallion from his pocket and hung the chain around his neck. "As ready as I'll ever be I guess."

"How do we even know that this is what we are looking for?" Nicole asked. "The energy could be coming from something else."

"There's only one way to find out," Ethan told her.

"Maybe we should go in with him," Sarah offered. "So we can at least see what happens, and that he is okay."

"I agree," Nicole frowned.

Dash shook his head. "This is something I need to do on my own. Imagine if I'm right ... imagine the possibilities."

"Yeah, imagine if you're wrong ... about any of it," Nicole came back, her voice angry and shaking.

Dash stepped closer to her and grabbed her hand. "You know you're my best friend don't you?"

Nicole nodded, tears flowing down her cheeks. "And you're *my* best friend, which is why I don't want you to do this."

"Don't be a silly girl. I'll be back before you know it."

Nicole didn't respond.

"I left you the recipe. It's in your desk at Ethan's office."

"Thanks," Nicole tried to smile.

"Just in case," he added.

Dash gave her a quick peck on the cheek before turning away. "Hey ... if I'm wrong I'll be back in a minute. If I'm right ... well who knows?"

They stood there watching as Dash disappeared into the cave. The minutes passed as they waited for him to return, but he didn't.

"Let's go in and see what happened," Nicole suggested.

"I don't know." Ethan was doubtful.

"If it is a portal, it won't matter because we don't have one of those medallions. But if something's happened to him in there, we need to find out," Nicole reasoned.

"She's right," Alec told them. "I'll go in and check it out. The rest of you wait out here."

Alec returned a few minutes later with a puzzled expression on his face. "It only goes back about four feet, and then it's just a rock wall."

"It must have worked." Ethan's face lit up.

"Yeah, but what do you think is going to be waiting for him on the other side?" Nicole's anger had returned.

"We'll wait around for a while to see if he returns," Alec suggested. "Even if he doesn't, I'm sure he'll find his way back sooner or later. There has to be a way back." Alec tried to comfort Nicole.

* * * *

Sarah stared up at the night sky. The way the stars twinkled against an abyss of darkness was magical. It was easy to imagine that as long as there was starlight, that radiance would keep evil from overcoming the world.

If only that were true - if only those heavenly lights could keep away the darkness that was winding it's way through her heart.

At first she'd been so sure it was Darrien that she'd seen at the rest stop, but after running the scene through her head over and over again, she was no longer certain. Maybe it had been a ghost, or just someone that resembled him. It was easy to make a mistake when it was so dark.

It could have been just some drifter using the restrooms as a place to sleep. She was still grieving. Maybe she just wanted it to be him so bad that her brain had made her believe that the person that she encountered was Darrien.

Sarah burrowed deeper into her sleeping bag in an effort to stay warm. Nicole slept only a few feet away. The guys didn't have a choice but to stay in the van. They couldn't be outside when the sun came up.

Closing her eyes, Sarah tried to fall asleep. Just as she was ready to doze off, a rustling in the underbrush brought her full awake. Sitting up, she stared in the direction she'd heard the noise. The moon was bright, but not really bright enough to make out much of anything.

Then she saw him, a dark silhouette against the moonlit sky. Sarah scrambled from her sleeping bag and started toward him. There was a chance that she was wrong, and the person was just some stranger getting his thrills by watching them sleep, but she didn't think so.

She could feel him - feel his presence. She could feel the essence of his being in a way that was only possible with someone that you loved so intimately, and so deeply.

As soon as she started moving toward him, he sprinted. Sarah started to run in the direction he'd gone.

"Darrien," she called after him. "Don't run away from me … please."

She followed him through the trees and out into an open - grassy meadow. He stopped, but he was still far ahead of her.

"Don't run from me," she yelled. "I will follow you to hell and back, if I have to."

"Why are you here Sarah? Who brought you?"

"We came here looking for the Place of Light … *Outerlands*," she told him. "I didn't know you would be here."

"You are fools! There is no such place. It is hell that you seek," he told her bitterly.

Sarah shook her head. "No Darrien."

She took a few steps toward him, but with every step she took, he would move further away.

"Stop," she shouted. "I think you owe me an explanation."

"I'm a monster Sarah … a real monster. The boogeyman that comes out of your closet at night," he laughed harshly.

"No, I don't believe you," Sarah told him, moving cautiously in his direction. She didn't want to risk him running again. There was simply no way she could keep up with him if he did.

"Don't come any closer!"

"Or what Darrien? Are you going to attack me?" she asked. "If you are the monster that you claim to be, isn't that what you would do?"

"Just go away Sarah."

The defeat and sadness in his voice were like shards of pain going straight into her heart.

"Why can't you believe in me Darrien? Why can't you believe that we can get through this, no matter what it is?" Sarah's voice splintered, her heartbreak coming through with every word. If she lost him again, she knew she would simply wither and die.

"Not this we can't."

Sarah took two more steps toward him, but again he started to turn away.

"Don't Darrien! Please don't turn away from me," she begged.

Another step and then she could see why he was running from her. She could see the hideousness of his deformity. Sarah willed herself not to so much as flinch or avert her eyes. She took another step toward him.

"Now are you satisfied that you can see me as the monster that I truly am?" Darrien turned away from her.

"You are an immortal Darrien. You will heal."

He shook his head. "We are flesh and blood. You know that. Your very existence is evidence of that."

"But ..."

Darrien cut her off. "Not the sun Sarah. The sun damages the cells that regenerate."

"Do you really believe me to be so shallow that this would matter?" Sarah asked angrily.

"You are fooling yourself Sarah," he told her in a low voice. "You would feel revulsion every time I touched you."

Sarah reached out to place her hand on the scarred flesh of his arm. "I love you ... what you look like doesn't matter."

Darrien shook his head. "Sarah, don't make this any harder than it already is."

"So now that you look different ... does that mean that you don't love me anymore?" Sarah asked him.

"No it doesn't mean that. I do love you. I will always love you," he whispered.

"Then prove it," she told him. "Hold me in your arms Darrien. Kiss me. I've been too long without you."

Slowly he turned to face her. Sarah slipped her arms around his neck and brushed her lips against his. Darrien pulled her close and kissed her. At first his kiss was tender and uncertain, but then his kiss turned to one of yearning.

When he pulled away, he placed his cheek against hers. She could feel the dampness of his tears ... the tears of a vampire.

Sarah's heart swelled with a love so complete - so pure that its light was far more brilliant than any light of heaven.

"Will you marry me?" Sarah asked him.

Darrien pulled back. "You're joking?"

Sarah shook her head. "No. I want to marry you tomorrow ... next week ... next month. I don't care when. I just want you to promise that you will be with me the rest of my life."

"I promise," he told her, his lips next to hers.

Sarah wanted no more words. She pulled him down with her into the grass of the meadow. Darrien was on her, kissing her hungrily as he tore away the barrier of her clothes.

"Are you sure," he asked.

"Very," she smiled.

As he caressed her body, Sarah felt herself drowning in her need for him - her love for him, and her desire to be possessed by the only man she would ever love. In that instant, she felt so much love and so much happiness, that she began to shake uncontrollably.

"Are you okay," he asked.

Sarah smiled. "I'll always be okay, as long as I'm with you."

As they made love, Sarah's heart was filled with everything that was good in the world. It was only in the arms of this immortal that she could feel such optimism. With their need sated for the moment, Sarah cuddled closer to him, her hand straying to the scars on his face.

Darrien stiffened.

"Don't," she told him. "I love you ... all of you."

Sarah put her arms around him and squeezed tightly. She made a vow to herself that she would eventually heal him. She would heal his body and his soul. What her love could not heal, magic would.

For the time being she was content. Tomorrow was another day, and there would be time enough to find out what happened to Dash, and to fight the evil that would descend on the world, but for now she was content to just be close to the one she loved.

Author

Lorraine Kennedy is a romance author of mixed heritage. Coming from a rich and diverse background spawned her love of history and an array of cultures. Lorraine has been weaving tales since she was a child, but it was not until she discovered Paranormal Romance that she was able to find a home that would fit well with her style of writing.

You can keep up on new released by Lorraine Kennedy by visiting www.lorrainekennedy.com

CPSIA information can be obtained at www.ICGtesting.com
Printed in the USA
LVOW041400031111

253389LV00001B/18/P